RAT BOHEMIA

SARAH SCHULMAN

RAT BOHEMIA

A DUTTON BOOK

DUTTON

Published by the Penguin Group
Penguin Books USA Inc., 375 Hudson Street, New York, New York 10014, U.S.A.
Penguin Books Ltd, 27 Wrights Lane, London W8 5TZ, England
Penguin Books Australia Ltd, Ringwood, Victoria, Australia
Penguin Books Canada Ltd, 10 Alcorn Avenue, Toronto, Ontario, Canada M4V 3B2
Penguin Books (N.Z.) Ltd, 182–190 Wairau Road, Auckland 10, New Zealand

Penguin Books Ltd, Registered Offices: Harmondsworth, Middlesex, England

First published by Dutton, an imprint of Dutton Signet, a division of Penguin Books USA Inc.
Distributed in Canada by McClelland & Stewart Inc.

First Printing, October, 1995
3   5   7   9   10   8   6   4

 REGISTERED TRADEMARK—MARCA REGISTRADA

LIBRARY OF CONGRESS CATALOGING IN PUBLICATION DATA:
Schulman, Sarah.
Rat bohemia / Sarah Schulman
p.   cm.
ISBN 0-525-93790-0
1. Lesbians—New York (N.Y.)—Fiction.   2. Family—New York (N.Y.)—Fiction.
I. Title.
PS3569.C5393R37   1995
813'.54—dc20   95-15475
CIP

Printed in the United States of America
Set in Cochin and Charlemagne

Designed by Steven N. Stathakis

"Stopping by Woods on a Snowy Evening" from The Poetry of Robert Frost, edited by
Edward Connery Latham. Copyright 1923 © 1969 by Henry Holt and Co., Inc. Reprinted by
permission of Henry Holt and Co., Inc.

For Jacqueline Anne Braun

ACKNOWLEDGMENTS

For reading my manuscript and offering comments I would like to thank Carrie Moyer, Bettina Berch, Beryl Satter and Jacqueline Woodson. And for letting me read aloud to her at any time, much love to Maxine Wolfe.

I'd like to thank my parents, David Schulman and Gloria Yevish Schulman.

For financial support during the development of this novel I would like to thank the Barbara Demming/Money for Women Fund, the Revson Program for the Future of New York at Columbia University, the Authors League Fund and the PEN Writers Fund.

Special thanks to my editor and friend, Carole DeSanti.

CONTENTS

Portions of *Rat Bohemia* previously appeared in *Diva* magazine (London), *By The Light Of The Silvery Moon* (Virago), and in *Frighten The Horses*. Materials were also used for two stage plays: *1984*, with Mark Ameen, directed by Rich Rubin, and *Killer In Love*, with Bina Sharif and Diane Torr, directed by Jenny Romaine. Both premiered in November 1993, at Performance Space 122 in New York City.

PART ONE

RAT
BOHEMIA

CHAPTER ONE

THE WORLD'S LARGEST RATS ARE THE CAPYBARAS, the web-footed denizens of the Amazon. Their hair bristles when they get angry and they are extremely hostile to humans. Even ones they know over a long period of time. There was a special series on capybaras in the Kuala Lumpur newspaper. My friend David sent it to me when he was on vacation because he knows how much I care about rats. The articles basically discussed the pros and cons of raising the animals for food.

Bandicoots, which is what giant rats are called in India, are not eaten. Originally they lived in the country but got too fat to climb the stalks of wheat. So, they traded places with the smaller city brand which then migrated to the country and wiped out the crops that the fat ones couldn't reach.

David is HIV-positive but he still had 600 T-cells when he went to China so we didn't have to worry that much. Once over there he went to Guangzhou and wrote to me about a rat-control campaign where the city published special recipes trying to get the residents to eat those rodents up.

He said he saw red lacquered ones, basted with honey and soy, hanging by their tails in the market. But, just like their American counterparts, all Chinese rats are not equal.

So, people generally complained about eating sewer rats which they considered only one step removed from eating sewage.

One night David slept out on the street in Chengdu and a rat bit him on the fingernail. He was relieved that it didn't get his blood, but surprised the animal chose nail instead of flesh. This was later explained to him by a madman he met on the streets of Guangzhou.

"Rats," said the madman. "They need to grind down their teeth or they die of starvation. So, they bite hard things. Preferably wood, bones, even people."

A few years ago the mayor of New York decided to cut back on rat extermination. He also cut back on streetlights. As a result, night increasingly meant these dark outlines of buildings surrounded by the scampering of eighteen-inch varmints. Ten million of them at least.

My best friend Killer and I spent a lot of nights that summer just walking around because we didn't have any money. I was saving up to move out of New York and Killer hadn't had a job in two years. She came over every night to eat and then we'd take a walk. She'd forgotten how to even look for a job. She'd forgotten how to sound employable on the telephone. One day I glanced over her shoulder at the Help Wanted pages of the *New York Times*, only it wasn't what you'd call *pages*. It was more like half a column.

One Saturday afternoon we saw a kid get shot in front of The Unique Clothing Store Going-Out-Of-Business Sale and the next day we watched a guy go crazy and throw glass bottles at people for twenty minutes. I've always wanted to shoot rats.

Killer and I are hardcore New Yorkers. But, when we were kids, the only homeless person you'd ever see would be a wino on the Bowery or an occasional bag lady. You never saw anyone sleeping on a subway unless they were coming home from the night shift. The streets were not covered with urine then. That was considered impolite. There have always been rats, though. I remember as a teenager watching them run around on the subway tracks while I was waiting for the Seven train to get me the hell out of Jackson Heights. But mostly, when I was a kid, rats were something that bit babies in a mythical faraway ghetto. You never saw them hanging out in the middle-class sections of Queens.

An average rat litter is twenty-two little ones and they can reproduce at the rate of six litters a year. Sometime in the 1980s I started to see them scampering regularly in the playgrounds of Central Park. Reagan had just become president and I held him directly responsible. Rat infestation felt like something the U.S. government should really have been able to handle. That's when I started thinking about getting a gun and shooting each one of them on sight. Picking them off the way hillbillies shoot squirrels.

That guy, last Sunday, who was throwing bottles? All he cared about was himself. His personal expression was more important to him than other people's eyes. That's the kind of attitude that makes this town a dangerous place to live. You never know when it can hit. The shooting in front of The Unique was more reasonable. It was just a bunch of friends killing each other. Don't have friends like that and it will never happen to you.

CHAPTER TWO

EVERY MORNING I GO OVER TO THE OLD VETERANS' Administration building on West Twenty-fifth Street and wait on line to go through the metal detectors. The crowd moves slowly so all of us look around at the lobby walls. They're covered with old World War II murals of white soldiers getting fitted for artificial legs by white nurses in starched caps. The women lift up the veterans' new legs and demonstrate how to use them.

Once I make it past the security guards, I have to ride up in the elevators with all the whacked-out veterans scratching and getting into fights. Mostly black and Puerto Rican with a sprinkling of white trash. They usually get off first, and then I ride up alone to the seventeenth floor where there is the Food and Hunger Hotline office. I walk through them to my office and then sign in at Pest Control, wasting about half the day unless I get sent out on a job.

When I am sitting in Pest Control, hanging out, waiting, I pay close attention to the goings on at Food and Hunger. I want to see everything I can. Everything. I want to be a witness to my own time because I've had a sneaking suspicion lately that I'm gonna live a lot longer than most of the people I meet. If I'm gonna be the only one still around to say what happened, I'd better pay close attention now.

Killer usually stops by the office at ten for coffee and peanut butter sandwiches. Then she checks in at a couple of restaurants to see if they need any prep cooks. I know for a fact that they're only hiring Mexicans and Israelis. Everybody knows Americans aren't good for restaurant work. They want to talk on the pay phone and give their friends free meals.

In the meantime she's living on forty dollars a week from watering plants for a couple of offices and boutiques. The rest gets paid by the Bed and Breakfast guests she hustles at those four-dollar cappuccino places. Mostly Swiss people or Germans. They think it's quaint. She gives them a bed and then tells them to make their own breakfast. Then she comes to the office to eat some of mine. We've been living this schedule for a long time already. It is one big fat habit.

You know one thing I don't like about homeless people? They ask you for a light and then hold on to your lighter for forty-five minutes blabbing on and on about some misfortune. The whole thing is designed to make it seem like they don't realize that they've got your lighter. But the fact is, they know they've got it.

My father always raised me to be extremely polite to black people. To say "Yes, sir" and "Yes, ma'am" and to feel sorry for the hardships they'd endured. Black and white never socialized together where I grew up—or anyplace I've ever heard of, for that matter. But I was raised with some kind of naive expectation that saying "Yes, sir" would take care of all of that some day. I was never expected to see my family's own stake in racism. How mediocre we really were and how much we depended on it to be able to put food on the table. I mean, how many white people would own cars today if merit was the only thing that mattered?

Killer was brought up to be a racist. One night I went over to her place to watch TV and her parents brought over some food. Next thing you know the news came on and it was all "nigger" this and "nigger" that. Her parents had these sharp teeth whenever they said that word. They scrunched up the skin around their eyes. It wasn't said calmly. Killer knows better but when she gets emotional, that's what she falls back on.

Like one time some Puerto Rican guy was beating up his kid in the hallway and Killer said, "Look at that low-rent over there."

"Shut up," I said. "You haven't had a job in two years. If you had enough patience to stand in line you'd be on welfare yourself."

"I'd be on welfare if it wasn't for the strength of the Eurodollar," she said as some blond couple rolled over in the bed. That was the way she looked at things.

God that summer was hot. There's that way that Puerto Rican girls sit close together on the stoops. They have skinny arms and those ten-dollar pink dresses. They smile and wear their hair long with a headband.

Every day homeless people come into Food and Hunger looking for food but they only get Contact Cards. I gave Killer one of those cards but she said the food they advertised wasn't nutritious.

One time, before breakfast, Killer walked me to work but she wanted to stop off at the Xerox store on Tenth Street that was run by some Moonies. They were clean-cut peculiar and wore polyester pants up to their necks.

"They give away free bread and free Chinese buns," she said.

When we walked in it was kind of slow and real hot. It stunk of Xerox fluid. The polyesters had a few day-olds sitting on the counter and a bag of day-old buns.

"Don't eat it," I said. "It's old pork."

"Hi, Killer," they said, handing her two loaves. Then they turned to me. "What about you?"

"I don't need free food," I said.

"Look," Killer whispered. "Take it. I need it. I'll give you a fresh one later. For your birthday."

"Okay. No, wait a minute. I don't want bread for my birthday. I want a colander."

"Do you think I need a professional portfolio?" she asked. Killer was still thinking about jobs.

"How is everything going?" Killer asked the Moonies, remembering to be gracious.

"We're having problems with rats," they said.

That woke me up.

"Do you have big ones?" I asked. "One-pounders?"

"Yep," they said.

"Did you put out poison?" Killer asked.

"Poison doesn't work," I said. "They're too strong. Besides, if you kill one that way it's just gonna stink up your place and bring maggots."

"Did you try traps?" Killer asked, trying to cut me off because she knew what I was about to recommend.

"Traps don't work," I said, ignoring her. "The rats are too smart. They spring the traps and get the bait."

"What about walk-in traps?" one of the Moonies asked.

"Too expensive," I said. "Doesn't work on a massive scale."

"Well, what do you suggest?" he asked.

"You gotta shoot 'em," I said. "You gotta get 'em one by one."

CHAPTER THREE

I WAS BORN RITA MAE WEEMS IN JACKSON HEIGHTS, Queens, New York City, U.S.A. on August 1, 1959. My father, Eddie Weems, fixed couches for Castro Convertible. My mother, Louisa Rosenthal Weems, was one of those hollowed-out blond beauties who made their way to New York via Thereisenstadt and then a displaced persons' camp. There are a lot of them still walking around. I see them on the subways now and then. But, in Jackson Heights where I grew up, they were a dime a dozen.

My mother smoked four packages of Chesterfields a day and died of cancer when I was ten. All my memories of her are stained nicotine yellow and accompanied by a deep, painful, hacking cough. Officially, I've given up on smoking. I rarely buy a pack. But some days I just do it. The privacy of a good smoke on a cold day.

Then, at night, I'll lie in bed clutching my breasts, my lungs, that hole in my chest where the burning smoke sits. My mind rolls over as I beg for redemption.

When I pray, I pray to the Jewish God. I pray to the patriarchal God—not an energy or a spirit—but that old white man with a beard sitting up there deciding things. My mother prayed to him. My grandmother prayed to him. And, as far as

I am concerned, that is reason enough. We exist together in that moment of panic where my thoughts turn up to the sky.

Judaism isn't that hard to understand. It all boils down to a few basic principles. There is one God. That is sort of the main belief. Second, but also important, is the idea that you can't worship things. You can't bow down before idols. I'm not saying that I think this way of looking at things is the only or best way. But, it is my burden and my gift because I inherited it from my mother. I don't care to know what the reason is that I am gay. But when it comes to being a Jew who only has one God, I know for sure that I was born that way.

My first job was cashier. Then I cleaned up a Catholic school cafeteria. All those girls in green plaid kilts with dusty white skin and matching white food. Instant mashed potatoes. Dishes of mayonnaise. A glass of milk. Instant vanilla pudding. By senior year I started working at J. Chuckles on Forty-second Street in Manhattan. There I earned enough money to buy a camel's hair coat.

My mother, Louisa Rosenthal, was born in Bremen and lost everything during the war. I, Rita, am named for her mother. My brother Howie is named for her father and my older brother Sam is named for her brother. Rest in peace.

She married my dad, a Catholic. But my mother was a person who could not care about things like propriety. She just went through the motions. What could the neighbors do to her now?

"Your mother liked the worst," my dad said a hundred thousand times. "She liked bratwurst, teawurst and knockwurst."

But he pronounced it "woist" like Huntz Hall in those

old Dead End Kids movies. It is the way most white people in Queens actually talk.

My mother was the most beautiful woman in the world. She had that fragile, German, movie-star sensuality. She had blue eyes and soft lips. Her mouth was shapely. Her hair was fine and bright. But her eyes were nothing, flat. That worked, though, for the completed beautiful victim look.

I have a photograph of her in a suit with shoulder pads, when she first came to New York and worked as a clerk at Woolworth's. She had thick lipstick and pale empty eyes. On the way to work some fashion photographer saw her on the bus and invited her into his studio to take a few pictures. Her face was slightly twisted. She held a sultry cigarette.

"Your mother was like Marilyn Monroe," my father said. "A real doll."

There are a few other photographs. Louisa and Eddie at Niagara Falls. Louisa and Eddie at Rockaway Beach. Louisa and Eddie eating a Kitchen Sink ice cream sundae at Jahn's Ice Cream Parlour. The kids are in that one too. Me, age three, sitting on my father's lap. Sam, age seven, happy, benign, acting just the way kids are supposed to act. Howie, age ten, looking to the side at the wrong moment, ice cream all over his shirt.

Here is one of the classic Weems family stories. It stars me, age two, sitting in the stroller at the German deli near the house where Louisa bought her teawurst.

"I'm not happy," I reportedly announced in a booming bawl.

"Why not?" Mr. Braunstein asked from behind the counter.

"I'm not happy," I repeated. "Because my daddy isn't here."

Where was he? Off in a car full of tools to some richer person's more expensive house in a better neighborhood of Queens or Kew Gardens or Forest Hills or some place in the city or out on the island, the North Shore. He held the nails in his mouth and spit them out into place. He carried a hammer in the sling of his work pants thinking about the good old days in the army during the war. Mr. Handsome G.I. Listening to the crap on the car radio. My dad knew all the songs.

Now, after a night of smoking I lie in bed, terrified.

"What am I doing with a cigarette in my hand?" I ask myself stupidly. "I've got to be out of my mind."

These days everybody is dying. Not just my mother. There's no illusion left to let a person feel immune. Invincible is over.

CHAPTER FOUR

I DIDN'T GET MY MOTHER'S HAIR. SAM GOT IT. MINE IS
blond and brown, sign of mixed race. Howie looks
even darker, real black Irish, and that's fine. But this in-
between kind of washed-out blah sort of shut me down in the
beauty department. I got blue eyes, true. But I also got blue
skin, really pink nipples that look paraffin-coated. No pubic
hair on the insides of my thighs. Thank God. Whenever you
see pubic hair in a movie or magazine the girl has never got it
down the insides of her thighs. But, in real life there are miles
of it out there. There is wall to wall carpeting in every household in America. Some girls get embarrassed and some act
like they never noticed. But there is a discrepancy between
most thighs and the ideal ones. Mine are kind of ideal.

I grew up. I got jobs. I moved far away from my destiny.
No husband. No night school. No screaming kids in snow-
suits and strollers. No trappings. Not trapped.

My first lover was rough, knowing, leathery. She held my
blue body. I was so young I didn't know what lovemaking was.
This woman was about forty, named Maria. She was sizable,
weighty, assuredly handsome. I had no expectations. I couldn't
give anything back. As we were doing it, I just couldn't be free.
Lovemaking seemed to revolve around the shifting of weight.

It had to do with climbing onto Maria's body. Her whole skeleton was involved. But when she opened my lips and put her mouth on my clitoris I couldn't react. It was too specific. The rest of me felt lonely. I was sixteen. I had no extra flesh. Maria masturbated in front of me. I sat between her legs staring like it was a television set.

After that I just started talking, blabbing on and on. I told her everything I did all day and what I was expecting to do tomorrow. I told her about every song on the radio and which ones I liked, which ones did not deserve to be hits. I told her about the time, when my mother was sick, that some strange accented distant relative I'd never seen before or since, took me to a store in Brooklyn to buy some clothes for the first day of school. I wore size 6X. I didn't understand why we had to go all the way to Brooklyn until we climbed up these shaky wooden stairs to the shop. The place was run by a group of friends who had all been in the same concentration camp. The clerks had numbers on their arms and screamed at each other like they were home in their kitchens. I was so small, their numbers were eye level and kept swinging past my face.

The second time Maria picked me up from work and made me keep on all my clothes. She was smart. Passing her hands over my young breasts, there was no direct touching. No contact. That was the first time in my life that I ever felt sexy. That was the first time I ever felt that thing. Desire.

Further down, I thought. *Please put your hands further down.* I got angrier and angrier as her hands stayed the same.

"You've got to ask for it," she whispered. She said it like a threat. "You've got to ask for what you want."

"Put your hands down there."

"Down where?"

"In my pants."

She lifted me onto her lap and fucked me fully clothed.

"*You* are a brave young girl," she said. "You're a darling girl. Keep your clothes on and it will always feel good."

The next and final time together, it was my turn to touch. It was an inquiry. I hadn't yet discovered shame. But Maria's cunt didn't open to my fingers the way mine had to hers. That's when I realized how trust shows in sex. It has nothing to do with how they act or what they say. It shows physically. I learned, instinctively, the telltale signs.

Being a salesgirl was a trap. That was clear from the start. Dad's new girlfriend Erica worked in sales and she was obviously trapped. The staff at J. Chuckles was trapped. The manager was trapped. Even the customers were trapped by the lousy selection of overpriced clothes. I knew that I was only seventeen. I knew I was young. This job was just a moment. It was just about saving up for a camel's hair coat. The coat was so dashing. It was substantial. It was something I had never seen before except on the back of a woman on line at Cinema One.

Saturday afternoons, after work, I went to Shield's Coffee Shop on Lexington Avenue and had an egg salad sandwich on rye. One dollar and five cents with a pickle on the side. I sat at the counter, exhausted, and stared out the window at the people on line at Cinema One. It was New York couples at Christmastime. The kind that went to foreign films. They had good taste. They weren't tacky little hitters from Queens. The girls in tight jeans and sparkle socks from my neighborhood spent their whole lives smoking Marlboros in front of candy stores. Their boyfriends died in car accidents or never got rid of the drug habits they'd picked up in Vietnam. Those girls wore blue eye makeup. They listened to Elton John and Yes and Black Sabbath at parties. They listened to *Tommy* by the Who, and Bach-man-Turner Overdrive. They did quaaludes with their older boyfriends and then eventually used needles and drank tequila right out of the bottle. They never saw foreign films. I hadn't either, but I would someday. That was the difference.

Outside the couples were standing in line. I ate my egg salad slowly, watching. Framed by the picture window was a distinguished older couple. The man wore a topcoat. His wife's hair was done. She linked her arm into his. They both looked ahead while discussing so they could watch and comment at the same time. Behind them stood a younger version. The woman's cheeks blushed pink. She had gold earrings. The younger guy wore a scarf and a jacket. His hair was long, hatless. Behind them stood two women, arms linked as well. They were engaged, laughed easily. One had to bend over slightly so the other could speak into her ear. And then something happened that changed my life forever. The two women kissed, romantically. The one nearest the window wore a camel's hair coat.

The next Saturday was Christmas Day. As soon as I could get out of the house, I took the Seven train into the city directly to Cinema One. I sat down in the virtually empty theater and watched the same foreign film those two women had watched. It was called *Cries and Whispers*.

In it, one woman touched another woman's face and kissed it. Another scene showed a different woman take out her breasts while a fourth laid her head on them. Then the first woman put a piece of glass in her vagina and rubbed the blood across her mouth. Throughout, a clock was ticking and people were whispering in Swedish. The subtitles said, "Forgive me." I went downstairs into a stall in the ladies' bathroom and masturbated. Then I went up and watched it again.

CHAPTER FIVE

WHEN I WAS A GIRL MY FATHER AND I WERE ALWAYS fighting. If he told me to get out and never come back, I'd be hovering on the front stoop for hours screaming to get back in. If he put his foot down and told me I couldn't go out, I'd do it anyway by going down the fire escape.

Our street, Eighty-second Street in Jackson Heights, was so quiet that me yelling or him yelling was enough for the whole neighborhood to hear. After a few people started complaining my dad got into the habit of calling the local precinct as soon as we'd get into a fight.

"Officer," he'd say into the telephone. "We have a girl here, out of control."

There were Spanish kids in Jackson Heights then but not so many as now. The Spanish and the whites never mixed. That really dates me. There was only one Puerto Rican guy who worked with my dad, but he lived up in the Bronx. There was a psychological divide then that was only violated, occasionally, by a passing beat-up Ford Falcon blasting salsa music from the radio. I didn't know that was the sound of the future. Rice and beans were what you'd have to eat if you didn't amount to anything. They were a threat. Not something delicious, orange and black with pork fat, hot sauce and fried plantains. Out on the street we only saw good-girl German Jews coming home from their violin lessons and lots of Irish kids blaming themselves for everything starting at the age of twelve. I knew a girl who lived two apartments up from ours named Claudia Haas and she started out as a good girl but ended up as a tramp.

My father was a rough guy. He'd already chased Howie out of the apartment and off to California somewhere to find peace and fortune. Dad's second girlfriend had dumped him about a year before and it was taking him longer than usual to find another one which also put him in a foul mood. So, when he tossed me out for the fifteenth time, I shrugged it off and went to the candy store to buy a pack of Salems.

There was Claudia Haas, tight jeans, tight V-neck short-sleeved sexy knit top. She was hanging out, a real hitter from Queens. She was drinking Mateus Rosé out of the bottle and listening to Seals and Crofts on WPLJ radio. The real truth is that Claudia Haas fell in love with me and I fell in love with her even though it wasn't possible on a warm Queens night in 1975 because neither of us knew what a homosexual was. It wasn't a word that was bandied about the newspapers then as it is today. Even I, who had already experienced it, had never uttered the word. I had never conceptualized myself that way.

Claudia and I talked together until late that night. We sat on cars, smoked cigarettes, listened to Yes do *Close to the Edge* and fell in love. Claudia's boyfriend wore his Vietnam army jacket, turned us on to Thai weed, drank beer, listened to Grand Funk Railroad, to War, to Average White Band and Janis Ian, to the Allman Brothers singing "Whipping Post" live at the Fillmore East, to Carly Simon singing "You're So Vain," to the Stones, Emerson, Lake and Palmer, Acoustic

Hot Tuna and the Dead. It was a different, stupid America. We hadn't yet given up trying to get over Vietnam. We reveled in our mediocrity. America wasn't nihilistic yet. We weren't all suffering.

That night, after partying, the sky was all mine, warm on my skin. I followed Claudia up to her parents' tiny apartment, like ours, four rooms smashed together into a purposeful square. Remove the walls and we're all head to toe, head to toe. Her mother had left the kitchen light on, illuminating a plate of *muhn kuchen*, invitingly untouched on the rickety table.

"Come on," Claudia whispered, leading me into the family bathroom where we spread out towels to lay stomach down on the cool tile floor.

"What's the green stuff?" I asked.

"Herbal Essence shampoo. Smell it."

It smelled good. She had all kinds of things, special kinds of hair brushes and sponges, powder. I never learned how to use products. Didn't even know where to begin, having spent my life staring at mothers with lipstick and hairstyles, panty hose — all those mysteries no one ever explained.

There's so much now that I wish I'd understood. But no one ever sat me down and looked me in the eye, lovingly, with information. To tell me that some things lead to certain other things and letting me in on the codes, shortcuts and signs. Everything about the future came to me in the form of threatened punishment. Or a silence surrounding my own wild imagination.

"Here, I'll brush your hair," she said, pulling it off the back of my neck.

"I looked at these at Field's," I said. "But I didn't know what they were."

The brush felt so good against my neck, her hand there too.

Then we lay back on the floor, whispering, passing back cigarettes and blowing the smoke out through the open window.

"I'm going to Queens College in the fall," Claudia said, feet up, straight blond hair cut back in a soft shag. "What about you?"

"I kind of stopped going to school," I said.

"What did your father say?"

"He hasn't mentioned it. I've been working at J. Chuckles in the city. Is Queens College really that great?"

"My sister's been there for three years. One more and then she'll move out. After that I've got the bedroom all to myself. I got wait-listed at two other places though, so the future is really unknown. Do you have a boyfriend?"

"Are you in love with Herbie?"

"Sure," she said. "You know what? He had this rubber last night. It said, *Put a tiger in your dot dot dot.* Everything's fine except there's one thing about him that I really hate."

"What's that?"

"When we're doing it, you know, balling? Sometimes he pushes my head down there because he wants a blow job. I get really pissed off. Don't tell me what to do. I'm not some Vietnamese girl who has to do what he says. It's not nice."

She rolled over on her side. I was used to the dark by now and the distant streetlights started to work for me, started to light us up. Then Claudia started singing.

"Du bist zaire ferucht. Du mus nach Berlin."

"What does that mean?"

"Don't you know German?"

"My mother forgot to teach us."

"It means," she said, brushing a piece of my hair back with her hand, " 'you are so crazy, you must go to Berlin.' "

I felt her touch me and I saw her do it as well. I saw a certain gentleness, a womanly softness, as though reaching out to touch me was the most natural thing. It was *of course*. But somewhere, barely perceptible, I detected an excitement. Something crackling.

"Fallink in luff again, nevah vanted to," she started singing. *"Vat am I to do? Cahn't help it."*

CHAPTER SIX

THE REASON THAT ALL OF THIS BACKGROUND INFOR-
mation had been on my mind was because I spent
most of last summer thinking about the fact that, frankly, I
have not made as much of my life as I would have liked. I
have never learned how to achieve. That's why I've been saving up to move out of New York. Florida might be nice. Learn
how to drive. Go swimming.

Working this job is a real downer except when we go out
for the kill. That's the best. But in the meantime, I have to sit
here with the crew from Food and Hunger and listen to them
make small talk. Especially that Mrs. Sabrina Santiago. She
almost always has a city worker attitude and therefore kicks
my butt psychologically and regularly. Everything is about
her territory and her ability to lord it over me. But she has
nothing to brag about since she moves real slow and wouldn't
say "How are you?" if it was worth a million dollars in food
stamps. These types of relationships and social encounters are
what has made me question my life.

Killer and I talk about this all of the time, about how we
are going to better ourselves. The problem with Killer is that
she's a pretender. She pretends that something is going to
happen when nothing is ever going to happen. Then, when it

is over, she pretends that something did happen when actually it was nothing. I love Killer. I don't mean to judge her but I have to.

It all goes back to that lack of information that has plagued me most of my life. Without instruction I had no inkling as to how things would work out. But once you get really burned, you become suspicious and resentful of those telltale signs.

Killer says I'm nagging her but she's got to understand what can be taken away from you if you're not realistic. Pretending is too contagious. I already lost one friend that way over the summer and I'm not gonna lose another. It was so damn hot. One-hundred-and-two degrees for eight days. The floorboards were hot. The metal faucets were too hot to handle. The refrigerators were groaning, couldn't keep up with the heat.

I crossed the street carefully, so blurry in my thinking that the speed and distance of cars was difficult to determine. The path to Joan's building was like every other block. Filthy. It stank of putrid rotting urine and three-day-old cooked garbage. Plus there's that oh so familiar smell of rotting rat carcasses, rat flesh. The other rats feast off of it for days. That's what makes them different from us. They sponge off each other's bodies even after they're dead.

I remember when Joanie got in a really bad way. We had a party for her but she was three hours late. Then she spent another hour in the bathroom. When her girlfriend, Siri, used to call up friends for money, they always gave it, but only in checks made out to the landlord or the phone company so their cash couldn't go up in smoke.

On the walls of the basement were photos of Joan and

Siri taken at different happy occasions. Joanie eating flan in Puerto Rico. Joan and Siri sitting together in a chair. Siri making a birthday cake. Nine people came to the memorial service. Siri was supposed to come but no one even mentioned that she didn't show up. I looked at the pictures for a while and for the millionth time ran through my memorial images of Joanie. Joan laughing. Joan sitting in the heat without a shirt drinking a wine cooler. Joan and Siri dancing. Joanie with a needle in her arm. Joan standing in front of a crack house on East Fourth Street. Joanie saying "You have to let me go." Joanie shot in the chest in a drug deal in Puerto Rico. Joanie, such a tiny little thing.

Someone had her diary from 1979 to 1982 when she first came to New York from St. Louis. I worked with her for a couple of summers in Youth Corps. She was the social worker and I was her assistant. So, how come I never knew that she was using drugs? I must have been pretending. Here's what she wrote in her diary.

I've been spending all of my money on heroin. I had to borrow forty dollars for food and ended up copping instead.

That was eleven years before her death.

In Harlem they have a kind of heroin called "Watergate." I shot it in Roger's front room in front of the TV. Then this show The Word Is Out *came on. It was about gay people standing up. I could see that we are ready to emerge. Long live PBS.*

No, Killer better grasp, right now, that if she's gonna sit around and deteriorate due to lack of realistic planning, then I'm gonna be on her case every step of the way. I can't stand to lose another thing.

CHAPTER SEVEN

MRS. SANTIAGO CALLED ME OUT OF MY SORROW-
ful reverie and asked if I would messenger something over to the computer store on Forty-third Street. Now,
I knew that she was supposed to bring that over herself because Food and Hunger doesn't have the kind of money to
buy a messenger service. I also know that Mrs. Santiago lives
in Bushwick, Brooklyn—which is in the opposite direction
from Forty-third Street. So, out of the kindness of my heart I
said *yes*. Then she made me stand there, freezing my butt off
in that central air-conditioning while she chats away on the
phone for forty-five minutes. City worker.

Of course I'm eavesdropping because I've got nothing
else to do and the whole conversation seems to be about these
storerooms filled with flour that the city got ahold of. But, all
of this flour doesn't do hungry people any good because most
of them don't know how to bake bread. Or, if they do know,
they've got no place to make it. Especially if you are a person
with a substance abuse problem. You will never find the time
to make bread.

Therefore, all this potential food was sitting there going
to waste. Mrs. Santiago was suggesting on the phone that
they could get all the new prisoners in all the new jails to learn

27

how to bake bread and they could bake up all this flour and distribute it already made. She was suggesting that, in the future, when they build prisons, they could include bread-baking facilities and kill two birds with one stone.

By the time she actually handed me the package and I got downstairs, I found out that Killer had been waiting around in the lobby because both detectors broke down and everyone was being searched by hand.

"Fuck that," I said and we both set off for the computer store.

Unfortunately we decided to take the subway which promptly got stopped between stations.

After about ten minutes the conductor's voice came on over the PA system.

"Attention passengers. Due to a police shooting at the next station we have been temporarily delayed. But we will now proceed with caution."

"Proceed with caution?" Killer asked. "What is this, *Stagecoach*?"

"What are we going to do?" I asked.

"Look," she said. "When we pull into the next station, duck behind the seats. You gotta get lower than the bench in case the bullets come through the window."

So, when the train eased into the next stop we ducked. But, we both kept sticking our heads up to peek because we wanted to see what was going on. Sure enough the place was swarming with cops and a bunch of medical personnel, all looking very tired and overworked. Then the guy across the aisle from us started to have a psychotic episode. He started meowing. At the next stop, Killer and I got off the train.

"Killer," I said as we walked uptown. "Tell me something. What the fuck are we doing? What are we doing with our lives? I think about this all the time now and I can't figure out what category I'm in."

"Category?"

"Yeah, I mean, I don't have any money but I'm not *poor.* I have aspirations but they're spiritual ones, not careers. I look around at how people are really living and I can't identify. But when I turn on the TV I don't understand that either. What the hell is going on, Killer?" I asked. "Who the hell do we think we are?"

"We're bohemians," she said.

"What?"

"We're bohemians. We don't have those dominant culture values."

"We're bohemians?" I asked, meekly.

"Yeah," she answered. "Ever heard of it?"

"Of course," I said, indignantly. "It's people who go to foreign movies."

I was identifying already.

"Look, in the past there were decade-specific names," Killer said. "Like hippies, beatniks, New Age, punks or Communists."

"What do we call them now?"

"That's the whole thing," Killer said, her black hair flapping carelessly back. "Nowadays it's not generational. Bohemians aren't grouped by clothes or sex or age. Nowadays, it's just a state of mind. Anyone with a different idea is IN."

We were standing by the front door of the computer store and Killer obviously wasn't planning to enter. So, we stayed out on the sidewalk and discussed existence like any New Yorker would do in our place. We were outside in that inside kind of way. There's weather and a sky at the top of the corridor. The walls were made of buildings and streets ran on like cracks in the plaster.

"But what about turn on, tune in, drop out, socialism and other social-outcast stuff?" I asked.

"Listen," Killer said. "In the fifties, the Beats, those guys were so all-American. They could sit around and ponder aesthetic questions but a cup of coffee cost a nickel. Nowadays, with the economy the way it is, you can't drop out or you'll be homeless. You gotta function to be a boho. You have to meet the system head-on at least once in a while and that meeting, Rita, is very brutal. Nowadays you have to pay a very high price to become a bohemian."

CHAPTER EIGHT

WHAT WAS I SUPPOSED TO SAY? KILLER TOOK OFF down Broadway and I walked into the air-conditioned computer store, bursting through to that other reality. The opposite of my heart. There were a lot of men running around like big overstuffed rats. Big ones, boring with stupid glasses and bad values. I stood on line waiting for my turn at the counter and what do you know? Right ahead of me is this really beautiful Spanish girl chatting with all the salespeople. She knew them all and they knew that she was really some character, but still likable. Plus, she looked really sexy. She had stylish cotton pants that ended halfway down her brown calf and black slippers and this loose cotton shirt that moved this way and that so you could see her belly once in a while. I knew this girl had spent half an hour in the dressing room of some department store twisting and turning to insure that her belly showed *once in a while.*

After another minute of watching I had a second layer of observation. This was the kind of girl who gestured big and talked big and showed her emotions big, but she wasn't really showing anything. All her actions turned out to be one big flirt. But, if you paid attention, as I did, it became obvious that she was flirting with no one. She was keeping all her real passion on reserve. That's how I knew she was a lesbian.

We started chatting about this and that and she was going into incredibly boring detail about computerland. Then she let me sit down next to her at the terminal and watch things come up on the screen. It was funny, everything on the screen happened quickly and so she happened quickly. The machine got her all geared up, constantly anticipating the next move, ready to jump.

She invited me out for a drink which turned into dinner which turned into her treat since I didn't have any money and she had about six credit cards. I knew right away that they were all overcharged and some day soon the loan shark would be after her. But, in the meantime she was sharp, tough and having as much of a good time as far beyond her means as she could get. That's when I knew she was Cuban.

"Cubans are the saddest people I have ever known," she said. "We're angry and can never be understood."

"The Cuba nobody knows," I said.

"On the other hand, we really like to live it up," she said, choosing the best things on the menu.

It was all about how rich her grandfather used to be and how poor her father is. But that was just one of the stories.

"In my town there was a terrible housing shortage. Every family was crowded together. It was very hard for gay people to find a place to have sex. Down the street from my mother's house was this gay man who had his own place. He had four small rooms occasionally to himself. Those nights different lovers would go to his house and find a room to make love. One night my sweetheart and I were making love in his house and suddenly we heard a noise outside. Some kind of political parade going by with lights shining through the window. We thought it was against us. Terrified, we rushed out into the center room and so did the other lovers. There we were, four couples, all men, Beatriz and me. We lay there silently, together, nude on the floor with our hands over our heads, waiting."

"Was it against you?"

"That's not important. I'm telling you about the bodies, like corpses, smelling of sex and then of fear. That's what I'm talking about right now."

"Why only tell half the story?" I asked.

"Because I don't know the other half or because it's none of your business."

She took me back to her apartment. An apartment in New York City tells many truths. It shows where you really stand, relationally. It shows when you came, how much you had and what kind of people you knew. Her apartment was lonely. It was cozy and she had good taste but so much was missing.

We both knew we were going to have sex but when you don't know the other person there is this big void of knowledge from here to there. You don't know how skittish they are. When they're going to object. Everything has to be cool, cool, cool. Her place felt like a motel which made the whole thing easier, sleazier, more romantic. A neon sign was flashing from across the street through the venetian blinds like some forties film noir. In fact, she seemed very glamorous.

First we smoked pot and then we smoked cigarettes while I watched her make preparations. She turned off the lights and lit candles and stretched out on the floor. I started thinking about all the times I'd been in situations like this one. All the times I'd been alone, together, in a poor apartment with a woman with a past and something that makes it all so stark. Like our bones are showing. Everything else fades in importance except this place, this secret place, this motel room and our certain, quiet longings.

CHAPTER NINE

WE START KISSING AND I'M LIFTING HER BODY onto mine. She's gorgeous. Within a few minutes I could tell from the way it was *my* hands around *her* waist and *me* lifting *her.* The way she's crawling on top of my legs, climbing on, that she was turning over to me, wanting to give up. That's one thing I knew about sex. Not sex with love, but just for the sake of it. Most people want one of two things. Either they want you to submit. Or, they want to get lost. They let you know which one it is right away. As for me, I don't have a particular sexual taste. I just like the part where she shows her desire.

When I reached down her pants and pushed inside her, this woman leaned back in my arms and said, "In this house we wear gloves."

"What?"

"In this house we wear gloves."

"What do you mean?"

"We wear latex gloves. You know, because of AIDS."

This woman had beautiful skin, like the beach, and our bodies fit. She was free and open, but not too open and she was sexy. She wanted to touch me. But I could not let her put on surgical gloves. I like to get off but I don't need to be fucked that badly.

"Well, I don't do that," I said.

"You never know," she said. "The virus is always mutating."

"I know a lot of lesbians," I said. "So do you."

She nodded.

"I've never heard of anyone who really got HIV sexually from another woman," I said.

"No, there's a case in Arkansas. My friend told me about it."

"There's probably a man or a needle lurking there somewhere," I said. "If lesbians were getting AIDS from each other, don't you think we would have noticed?"

"Better to be safe than sorry," she said.

The situation was starting to get testy.

"Look," I said. "I have an idea. You do what you want and I'll do what I want. Okay?"

So that's how it went. I fucked her and sucked her and reached behind to that place you can only get to with your fingers. Who knows what it looks like? Each time that it was my turn she held me and guided my hands to my own cunt and then held her hands over mine while I masturbated. That happened a couple of times. When she was ready to let me have it, she guided my hands there instead and put her hands over them. It was so weird, it was sexy, but there was also too much fear going on in the safest place. That place between our bodies.

I looked at this woman. I looked at her homosexuality. I watched it. I identified with her. Her nipples stood up under my fingers. Her ass fit in the palm of my hand. Her clitoris filled my mouth. Her hair was black and soft. We smoked, like lovers do, her on her back in the flashing neon light. Me, caressing her chest, smoke passing back to her and then back to me.

"This feels like a forties movie," I said. "Or a forties pickup, somewhere in Dayton, Ohio."

"Well, obviously you're the lounge singer," she said. "And I'm the New York bohemian just passing through."

"A real live bohemian?" I fluttered coquettishly. "Tell me, what's New York really like?"

"If this was the forties we'd be . . . we'd be . . ." She took another drag. "We'd be exactly who we are today. Our kind never changes. We're the international, eternal bohemia."

I put my white hand on her brown stomach. She looked like a little boy, like a Mexican film star, like flesh.

"No matter what goes on out there," she said, "we always do the same thing. We smoke pot, we have sex and we talk bullshit because we like it."

The venetian shadows flashed across her breasts.

"I know you want a drink of water," she said, holding the glass to my lips.

CHAPTER TEN

I HAD BEEN DISPATCHING ALL MORNING AND TALKING rats seriously with Mrs. Santiago.

"I know rats," she said, big like a Buddha in her office chair.

She never left that chair. She never even went to the bathroom. When it was time for lunch she just groaned, bent over and pulled out a paper bag from her bottom desk drawer.

"Before I got a desk job I was a case worker for the city. I used to have to go out in the alleys to wake up the sleeping homeless and invite them to shelters."

"What kind of program was that?" I asked.

"You remember," she said, patting back her nice, neat bun. Rearranging the photos of her grandchildren. Moving her glasses to the end of her nose and peering over the rims before completing her sentences. All of this designed to measure how much she owned you. Mrs. Santiago was so bureaucratic she wouldn't even gossip efficiently.

"You remember back a couple of mayors ago when they were inviting people in? Well . . ." She straightened a pile of papers on her desk, flipped through them listlessly and then straightened them again. "Well, when I'd walk into those alleys in the dark of night and shined my light I'd see thirty rats scampering all over the Dumpsters. Did you know that a rat can jump six feet from a standing position?"

"No," I said breathlessly.

"That's right. So, when you shine that light on them, you'd better be more than six feet away. Some of those people sleeping in the alley would have pieces missing from their arms when the rats just leapt up and grabbed their flesh."

She turned back to that same pile of papers, straightened them, slipped and straightened them again.

"Nice desk job for me," she said. "I only work at a desk."

Then I got a call from an on-site worker to bring down a big empty cardboard container to the corner of Astor Place where an assassination team was trying out a new, low-cost method. They were about to go on a lunch break so I didn't need to be there for three or four hours. So, I gave Killer a call to see if she would help me carry the container down to the Village. But David answered the phone instead.

"David, what are you doing at Killer's house?"

"I had to use her bathtub. My building hasn't had hot water for a week and I'm too stinky to be cute."

"Then, what are you doing?"

"Nothing."

"Want to accompany me on a walk downtown and make your contribution to a vermin-free New York?"

"Okay."

"See you soon. Dave?"

"Yeah?"

"You'll love it."

CHAPTER ELEVEN

O N THE WAY OUT OF THE BUILDING, I HAD TO PASS gauntlets of starving people begging for money for drugs or a roll. It's like now you have to pay a toll just to wait for the light. Sometimes it makes me feel guilty for wanting things—like my secret desires for a VCR. Other times it makes me want to walk inside some cafe somewhere and order something really decadent—like scallops. Something completely uncalled for.

As I walked to meet Dave I remembered the last time I went to a restaurant. I wasn't hungry. I had groovy coleslaw with orange peel and sesame seeds in it plus lemonade. It took three hours to eat. The girl wanted to kill me. She kept staring at my table, glaring, trying to burn me out of my seat. It was so cold outside that day I didn't have another choice. I was so fat that day my stomach was exploding. Every man on the street had to comment on my hips and every woman had to look at them and be glad hers weren't that way. My plate of coleslaw felt like a plate of lard. My lemonade was lard too.

That place had one of those old-fashioned ketchup hold-ers—a red plastic tube with a nipple on top. In that context it meant more than nostalgia. It meant nostalgia for your par-ents' nostalgia. There is a kind of loneliness that is solved through naked TV watching and late night talking to no one. I don't have a TV so I miss this opportunity and instead have to pace my tiny bedroom or look out windows at stillness in the dark. Can the smell of coffee keep you awake? That's what I wondered in that restaurant and then had to order some. Black tastes so thin. Like watered down hot scotch. It's bitter like a cigarette-stained tongue. Haven't had one of those in a while.

At Food and Hunger they talk about food a lot. One of our regular discussions is when everyone tells their favorite meal. Mrs. Santiago goes into this long rapture.

"First appetizers and then an open bar," she says. "Like you have at a fancy wedding or at the mayor's luncheon three years ago. Campari and tonic, about six of them. Then I like little shrimps in coconut milk, teriyaki beef, meatballs in a bowl made of bread, caviar and olives. After that, the fish course. Fish with sauce, and a baby chicken stuffed plus mashed potatoes and sausages. Then, an individual pastry with berries, strawberry ice cream and strawberry sauce. Then coffee."

David's favorite meal is a whole other thing.

"I choose yam cakes in spicy sauce," he said. "Spinach with dried fish flakes, marinated seaweed with minuscule whitefish in vinegar, potatoes with sugar and pork, tofu soup."

The guard at the metal detector's favorite meal is "Steak, well-done with steak sauce. A baked potato. A beautiful salad with Thousand Island dressing. Wine. Courvoisier VSOP."

My father's favorite meal is "Sweet and sour pork, pork fried rice, good beer and a fortune cookie, plus pineapple for dessert."

Mine is meat, with fruit and pineapple for dessert plus

wine. Homeless people say chicken, juice, fried rice, a sandwich, broccoli, corn, a grape.

When I asked Killer about her FM (favorite meal) she
suggested "A catered affair, wholesome and healthy. No
cheese. A broiled garlic cut in half so it looks like a pomegran-
ate. Broiled carrots, roasted peppers—red and yellow. The
best combination is to take a carrot and put it in curry sauce.
There would be three dips. Then people would walk around
with trays with little spinach pies and unidentifiable vegetables. Then there would be this thing called *tartettes*. The
waiter would keep coming over to ask 'Would you like a
tartette?' Stuffed mushrooms with, what's that called again?
Eggplant. Tiny little roast beef sandwiches. Two pieces of
chicken on a really hard piece of toast. In one hand everyone
would have a glass of champagne and in the other they'd have
a steamed artichoke. Think how beautiful the conversation
with those green paws raised high in gesture."

Sure, Killer had a great imagination all right, except
when it came to finding a place to live. She couldn't imagine
her way out of that slum. Killer's house is a good example of
urban blight. To get there I first have to walk past a rat-
infested vacant lot where some homeless have shanties. Day
or night the rats gallivant freely. They've never known fear.
These are rats who think that the world loves them that way,
that this world is *for* them. People bring them garbage like it
was TV dinners on a tray. Then they scamper, do aerobics
and whine.

When I approach that corner I get really tense, like a
foot soldier on the banks of the Mekong Delta. I scan the
sidewalk thoroughly and then try to race past as quickly as
possible. If a piece of paper or a plastic bag should suddenly

blow out of the sea of rats, I'll jump ten feet and scream. Later on I'll be clammy and pale, as though the actual monster ran across my bedsheets. And when the real ones do surface they are huge and deformed with tumors and other disfigurations. They get out in the middle of the sidewalk slowly and then lumber over to the garbage cans. Everyone's out there nibbling. When a car turns down that street its headlights illuminate them, swarming like larvae on old cat food. But they don't fear headlights. They just keep on. Then you get to Killer's house.

CHAPTER TWELVE

DAVID IS ONE OF THOSE MILD-MANNERED, BALDING kind of young men who only get creepy looks on their faces when talking about someone's big dick. Then he smiles, devilishly and his voice cracks. Otherwise he's the kind of guy I would have married if I had married a fag. Now he's down below two hundred T-cells, so I'm starting to worry. I love him and I hate him.

When I start to separate those feelings it is a real truth-teller about me, about what a cold person I can be. When I really face how I feel about David I see myself in a very unpleasant light. I see things unpleasant to convey. Like how angry I am that he never thinks about me. How angry I am that he's dying and so has a good excuse. How afraid I am that if he wasn't dying things might be exactly the same way. How ashamed I am that he is dying and I am only thinking of myself.

"Hey, Dave?"

"Tired," he said. "Can't sleep. Stayed up late last night trying to read Muriel Starr's new book."

"Good and Bad?"

"Yeah, everyone's reading it. Couldn't get past the first few chapters. Too closety. I just lay awake in bed for hours twiddling my thumbs."

"Where're you just back from this time?" I asked him as we walked down Eighth Avenue.

"San Francisco," he said.

"And . . . ?"

"No rats," he said.

I already knew that.

"It's so different," he said. "You walk out the door and there are three different kinds of trees, each with flowers of a different color. Yellow, red, white. Then there's another tree with little hanging plants that look like a string of bells. But, actually, they're petals. No rats, drug dealers or urine-soaked sidewalks in every neighborhood. It's all confined to a few, so just by walking you can actually get away from it and have time to have feelings and other emotions. You know, Rita, living daily in very hostile circumstances isn't good for us."

"Makes sense."

David is very concerned about being remembered. I'm concerned about remembering because, after all, I'm going to be left behind. People we know die all the time and there is really no way to react. What can you do? Freak out every day? Dave brings memory up all the time. I can see how appalled he is at how little any of us react to AIDS deaths. He's focused a lot of worry on being forgotten. That's one of his greatest motivations for going on trips and writing us letters. Continuing to make new friends and building relationships is one way to ensure his legacy.

We went half-time down the avenue. Dave was beginning to walk slow. I knew that the trip was hard for him physically, but whatever the cost was made up for spiritually when he realized he was going to make it the whole way. I could see he was starting to get that peripheral neuropathy where the nerve endings in your legs swell up. He called it "tendinitis."

"The Castro in San Francisco is the Valley of Death," he said. "There are sick people everywhere. Some are in their last moments and are being rolled around in wheelchairs. Others are just minimally decrepit, thin with ruddy medicinal complexions. The word AIDS is everywhere—on signs in newspapers. There is no pretense that it does not exist. That's what I noticed most, the lack of denial. I don't believe in denial. I think I'm joking. Everything I know to be true in my secret homosexual world is acknowledged publicly there. It's frightening, disorienting. Freedom is so unfamiliar.

"Here in New York AIDS is still a secret. When people get really sick they're embarrassed and so crawl into their apartments and die. They feel defeated and no one is there to help them get down the stairs. Only the drug addicts are out there on their canes. The formerly beautiful homos just lie in bed waiting for God's Love—We Deliver to bring a hot meal and then spend the rest of the evening throwing it up."

When Dave talks about his death, I act as though it is without question. I act almost blasé or at least one hundred percent accepting. I try to be relaxed. I'm used to it. I've also noticed that I don't mind getting closer to a person when they are dying of AIDS than I would usually get if they were living normally, men that is. That intimacy is worth a great deal to me.

By the time we got down to Astor Place, Dave was totally exhausted. He sat right on the sidewalk like it was a fat Persian rug. You could see how badly he wanted to go to sleep. I just let him be but kept one eye out at all times, casually, while focusing primarily on the scene down there. The work crew was trying out this new technique, and it was pretty disgusting. I hadn't seen a technique so blatantly gross before.

Two guys in regulation blue uniform jumpsuits had dug holes right around Peter Cooper triangle right in front of Cooper Union art school. Then they filled the holes with some kind of noxious water or poison. As the rats scampered to the surface, the guys hit each one over the head with shovels until their skulls caved in. It was so primitive. Like Fred Flintstone and Bam-Bam go hunting. That's no way to get a rat population the size of ours, I thought. It's not efficient. But, in five hours, the guys had killed at least one hundred and eighty that way. That's what they needed the barrel for—to throw away the carcasses. The funniest thing was that all the art students were standing around staring but none of them took a picture. Not a movie, not a sketch. Too busy being surprised, I guess.

CHAPTER THIRTEEN

I WAS READING A BOOK CALLED *LEAVES OF GRASS*. IT WAS all about the way people felt during the last century when Brooklyn was its own city and you had to take a boat to get there. I guess those Brooklynites stood on deck and watched the green grass of their homeland waving long and luxurious in the sun. Compared to the shit of New York, Brooklyn seemed like a forest.

Today you have to take the D train to get there. It sails right over one of the most beautiful stretches that America has to offer, that highway between the two boroughs where you fly off the bridge watching both sides through that twisted wire weaving. It's like the sinew under the skin of a body-builder in Chelsea. There's the black water and the blue sky and Wall Street where all the rich people of the officially beautiful world sit. On the other side are the projects where the saddest and most dangerous beautiful people of the unofficial world exist despite crime statistics, poverty graphs and the neglect quotient.

One night I was walking over to see Killer at her place on Avenue C and Seventh Street. I was crossing Avenue B and a Puerto Rican boy about fourteen, already with a mustache, started talking to me.

"Hi."

"Hi."

I always say "hi" believing it is an intermediary to death.

"The cops are at the brick man's," he said, warning me and flirting. Nothing is more attractive than a fourteen-year-old boy who holds the key to your death.

I ignored him, not knowing what he meant, until I got halfway down the block as the police were pulling away from the laundry. It was the only store on the block and was freestanding between two vacant lots. There were three churches—one black, one Latin and one evangelical white. But, commercially, only the drug business can survive on that block.

When I got to the storefront I could see that the police had raided the Laundromat and were now driving away. Just as they took off, before they got to the end of the block, coincidentally at the same moment that I was passing, all the junkies who had been hurting for their drugs, flocked back to the laundry. They came running back like there was a cracked piñata and candy for all. Then, after years of practice at unemployment, welfare, shelters, methadone and food stamps, they got in an orderly but panicky line while some guy sold heroin from the top of the stoop. The girls in that line were about fifteen years younger than me. Their hair was still long and black. One wore a stylish red beret. They lined up back to front like refugees in *Life* magazine waiting for rice. They held out their hands, palms up, waiting to catch their drugs. You can't see this from the Brooklyn Bridge.

Later, I was so disappointed that the Puerto Rican manboy would think I was buying heroin just because I'm white. It means I've failed. Is that what white people do in poor neighborhoods? Is that the only thing we do? Guess I don't look like a social worker, drug dealer or TV camera crew. I just look like a girl who wants to get high. Why else would I ever be here? Frankly, I'm too embarrassed to even consider being a junkie. I wouldn't want to ruin my reputation with others. I'd be afraid of what they would think.

Killer was happy that I finally arrived at her place because she had a psychodrama going on. She had had sex with some girl and now that person wouldn't call her back.

"She was really sexy," Killer said. "She wore those boxer shorts for women that have some man's name written on them."

"You mean Calvin Klein?"

"Yeah, that's it."

"So, why won't she call you back?"

"You know, Rita. You know how it is. Some people, you call them and they never call you back. Even if they've known you for a long time. I'd like to call those people up and say, *Listen Mack, if you ever call me I will call you right away. If I call you, I want you to call me back. Don't snub me or I'll kill you. Don't snub me.* Of course you can't go around saying *I'll kill you* to people or they'll never call you back. Plus, they'll tell other people you said that and then the others won't call either. The murderous intention has to be simply but subtly understood."

Killer went on and on about that girl but I was preoccupied. So, I just kicked back and had a beer while she rattled ahead. When you're drinking a beer *and* smoking a cigarette, there's no need to look for an ashtray 'cause bottle tops are lying around the table, right near where you put your feet. I wish I could dispose of memories. What good are they? Just a yearning for something that didn't happen and something sweet that was never said. It is an inventory of voids. Where is my mother? Why did she desert me?

CHAPTER FOURTEEN

D AVE CALLED ME UP TO SEE IF I WANTED TO WATCH
a movie. But, when I got over there it turned out to
be a stack of videos of all of our dead friends and then some of
his dead friends who I never knew. We watched them say and
do very ordinary things. Some of them were alive so long ago
that their clothing and haircuts were out of date. One guy,
Roger, seemed so far away. Then I realized that we had gotten older but he never would. Roger would always be young.
There were a few scenes of couples who were both dead.
Dave and I watched them acting out their sick couple dynamics. What a way to be remembered.

I almost never think about these guys unless I see someone on the street who looks like one of them. But David
wanted to talk about them. He would go on and on about who
was in love with who and who said what to who. The thing is,
he is going by a very outdated definition of what history is. He
was still pretending that history is the passing down of anecdotes from one set of friends to another. When they're all
dead there is no more continuity of the generations. I'm the
one who's going to be left and have to do all the remembering
and frankly, I'm never going to tell those anecdotes to anyone.

Right now, when I think of all my AIDS dead, one of the

things they all have in common is about forty conversations just like the one Dave and I had, where each guy talked about death in his own way. Later, they get sick and die in very predictable patterns. Let's face it, this death, itself, is no longer extraordinary, emotionally, to me.

David sat there and told me his most private thoughts about this death. While he was talking, I did exactly what I'd done forty times before which is to very matter-of-factly refuse to pretend that he's not going to die. In the meantime, what I had to say paled in comparison to his experiences but I'm the one who's gonna be left behind again. Doesn't that have a meaning too?

"When Victor died," Dave said, "I asked Steve what he remembered of their thirteen years together and he said that all he remembered was piles of Victor's shit from changing his diapers for two months. Rita, how do I ensure that my friends don't remember me like that?"

"You could tell us it's okay to hire a nurse," I said. I know that is not what I was supposed to say. I was supposed to say "Of course we'll remember you, Dave. You know that."

But I have said it so many times before and it wasn't always completely true. People fade. They become represented by a feeling. There are men in my life who have died and I can't remember their last names. Batya something's brother Jonathan who died in 1982. We went to a performance together once and he was skinny and miserable. He kept saying "But I wasn't promiscuous."

I mean, I will remember Dave, but I don't know for how long or in what way. I still remember Jonathan, somehow. Besides, sooner or later someone is going to have to hire a nurse and it is better to get that squared away so there is less guilt later.

One thing I know for sure is that AIDS is not a transforming experience. I know that we tend to romanticize things like death based on some kind of religious model of conversion and redemption. We expect that once people stare down their mortality in the mirror they will understand something profound about death and life that the rest of us have to wait until old age to discover. But that's not what happens. Actually, people just become themselves. But ever so much more so. If they took care of things before diagnosis, they take care of things afterwards. If they were selfish and nasty, they go down that way.

The public discourse on AIDS is getting more twisted by the minute. So many want to believe that there is some spiritual message at the core of this disaster — something we all can learn. That makes it more palatable, doesn't it? That makes it more redemptive. We all know the only good homosexual is a dead one but if we can prove that we're getting some kind of benefit out of our own destruction then maybe straight people will have a little more pity. But facts are facts. There is nothing to be learned by staring death in the face every day of your life. AIDS is just fucking sad. It's a burden. There's nothing redeeming about it.

Transformation is not the only misunderstood idea going on around this plague. Another one is CURE. There is no cure but everyone is out looking for it. Only, they've got a picture in their minds of something that could never be and so long as they cling to that clean concept it will never be found. The cure is not going to be some pill. It's not going to be one simple object or one simple act that a person just has to follow so that their KS will go away. There is no cure. There are just certain strange combinations of beliefs, acts and events that help some people feel better under some circumstances for some certain length of time. But there is no way to know why. Even when something comes along that helps some people feel better for some length of time, everyone poo-poos it because it is not THE CURE.

My friend Ronnie LaVallee said that the reason he felt better when he took some useless drug was because it was his father who found out about it and told him to try it, thereby proving that his father actually loved him. So, why didn't the newspapers announce the next day that parental kindness helps people with AIDS live longer? Because that's asking for more than people can do. Love our gay children? Impossible! We just want a pill. It's easier.

Every fag I've ever loved has had extermination hanging around his neck. How can that make for an equal opportunity at fate? Thank God pure mutuality is not my prerequisite for relationships. If it was, I wouldn't be able to talk to anybody except one or two dykes sitting on park benches watching the rats.

I love the Viet Cong, because that's the kind of American I am. I'm an UnAmerican. I believe that ninety percent of the people can be wrong at the same time. Your entire family can be wrong and you might be the only one who is right.

QUESTION: Is it better off, in that case, to be wrong?
NO. That's the patriotic way. Don't do that.
BE RIGHT.

Because, the way I figure it is that if I make my contribution to truth, some Rat Bohemian down the line will notice and appreciate it. She'll be sitting in a city strewn with

rats and rat carcasses and will come across my petite observation. That's the most amazing relationship in the universe.
The girl on rat bones who knows that she is not alone. She is
not American.

PART TWO

1984

CHAPTER FIFTEEN

I F YOU SOUND ONE NOTE OVER AND OVER AGAIN IT
becomes a note of alarm. Up until this moment two
things were absolutely certain about my life. *I'm broke* and *I
have my own way of looking at things.* That combination adds up
to a life that is simply worth it. But now, being infected is really lonely. You're just alone. And I'm one of the few who is
open about it.

If I'm gonna have sex, sometimes I'll tell them. But, if I
think he's the kind who will reject me, I won't say anything.
Or, if I'm the one getting fucked, which I usually am, I figure
it really doesn't matter. Some people say only the humpy guys
have it. The ones who couldn't get sex are running around
fine. Only the ugly will survive. But, when I get ready, over
my first beer, I look around the room and wonder who else
among the guys standing there is like me.

The bartender at the Tunnel Bar is one of my best
friends. If I see some cute guy I'll say "He's nice."

"She's got it," he'll say.

That means I'm supposed to immediately lose interest.

My friends, the men I know from going out, they pretend
they haven't got it but I know that many of them do. I'm not
angry at them. I'm angry at myself. I got it in 1984 when I

should have known better. But I guess I've always had an ambivalent relationship to living. Those of us who kept unabashedly fucking after the siren went off, those of us still alive and willing to talk say it was so exciting.

"I wouldn't have taken one less dick," a dead friend once said.

Of course it is just a virus and science isn't worth feeling guilty about. But I can't stop recalling those costumed gents getting off to the danger of fucking when you know you could die. What a turn-on. In a way it makes sex more than it really is, which is just a part of life, like a shower and a meal. Is having an orgasm in a dark room in a deserted part of town the principle most worth constructing your life around?

Yes.

No one can deny that, after all, there is something about desire that makes men treat each other like meat and love it. Goodness and badness have nothing to do with it. Desire can't be decided. But there is also that strange combination of camaraderie in nelly machismo. It is what the literary critics would call *fabulous realism* if they weren't too stupid to notice.

I know who gave it to me. It wasn't some leather-clad fireman stepping out of a tub of warm shit at the Mineshaft only to be fisted by a CPA called "Daddy" before sticking his dick up my ass. It was just this forty-year-old Italian guy I met on the street in 1984. He took me home to his apartment in Chelsea and right after he shot I thought, *I bet I just got AIDS.*

First, Sex Positive was the movement. Now, it's a sex movement. Sex, sex, sex. There's a lot of copulating going on out there. It's all come full circle back to 1984. Apocalypse Now! Paradise Now! Apocalypse Now! Paradise Now! It's either complete denial of the virus or complete acceptance. No one does safe sex all the time. No one outside of New York or San Francisco and even in those meccas it is easy to avoid. You can see it in the eyes of the young. They're sick of us being sick and just want us to die off already so they can have sex. But they won't wait that long. So the new wave of sex can eliminate that middle ground of decision where some young guy's expectation of a future is revealed. He doesn't expect to have a future. He doesn't even know what it would look like. What does a fifty-five-year-old gay man look like? A handsome one I mean. I look around the clubs at all those guys I've never met and know I won't be there to say, *Remember when.* I won't be there to say, *Didn't you used to go to Sound Factory about fifteen years ago?* I won't be around to finally fall in love.

The other guys I know must be thinking these same thoughts. They must be. But whenever it does come up it's always clichés about positive thinking or else some stockbroker bragging about his imported pharmaceutical like it was rock cocaine. It's a man thing. We don't like *intimacy.* We'd rather talk to our shrinks or brush it off. Dykes have the reverse problem. They're so intimate they go to the bathroom together. Straight people are the most pathetic of all. I've never seen such a miserable group of people in my life. They don't know anything about themselves.

Is getting fucked an act of heroism? It is if you're in the closet, if it's illegal, if your family will treat you worse than they do their houseplants. It is if you have HIV and they're telling you to just roll over and wait to die. But is prowling by night with the scent of sweat on your dick enough to make a fag into a hero? Last night I saw two old leather queens strolling down the street. *You bastards,* I thought. *You never loved men enough to let them fuck you. That's why you're alive today.* I think there is something stupid about men who have never been penetrated. You can see it in their eyes like glaucoma.

But cock and balls are easy to talk about. *C'est facile.* The real Achilles' heel of every Achilles is *LOVE.* That's the hugest unspoken fag issue of the day. Last summer I went to Fire Island, smoked a joint and walked down along the beach. Waves of perfect, white gym bodies kept coming at me like organic vegetables at the farmers' market. Only the best. Each one climbs up the Stairmaster every day because if his body isn't perfect no one will love him. Then what do all these queens cry about over their fifth martini? The fact that no one loves them.

This summer everyone is putting Nair on their chests to remove all the hair. They want to be boys again, pure. Thousands of hairless, gleaming, waxed, bionic men strutting around like a bunch of cars. The whole place felt like a parking lot.

Once a week or so I'll go over to Crow Bar on Tenth Street where boys flirt with clean-cut scrub-brushed clones of themselves. Everyone looks clean. Short hair, white T-shirt, clean jeans, pierced ear, collegiate. We're trying out for the Varsity Squad because clean boys don't have it. Only the dirty ones have it. So, I'll talk to some wide-eyed young queen who went to Vassar or Brown or some Euro-trash passing in East Village drag. We look into each other's eyes, feel the heat pass between our pumped-up gym chests. We both know for certain that the other one's underwear is clean. For that moment I don't have it and neither does he. AIDS is just a state of mind, sometimes. If you don't have to have it twenty-four hours a day, why do so?

I have this theory about HIV. I think there is good HIV and bad. Bad is what I've got. I can tell because my T-cells are plummeting. What I wouldn't give for two hundred T-cells. When I first went to the doctor I went to see Dr. Joseph Sonnabend because he is the best-known and most well-loved AIDS doctor. He's known for thinking that AZT is poison. He gave me a prescription for AZT. Someone explained that he probably wanted to give my T-cells a boost, try to get them back over two hundred, and that he would take me off it after three months, which is exactly what happened. Eight months ago.

My kind of HIV is the killer kind. It's killing me. But there are other guys walking around with HIV who never seem to get sick. Eight years, nine years, no symptoms. They've got the good kind. It occurred to me that if one night I can meet the right Mr. Clean and we can keep our minds AIDS free, maybe he will pump me full of the good HIV. Maybe it will neutralize my infection and I'll never have to worry again.

CHAPTER SIXTEEN

THE PHONE HAS BEEN RINGING ALL DAY. THEY KEEP ringing and hanging up. Ringing and hanging up. I know who it is. It is my mother. My parents are trying to kill me.

They don't call regularly. They call on a whim. They might be sitting around the house one Sunday afternoon, breakfast is done. The paper is done. Nothing to do for an hour before taking in a movie. *Hey*, my mother will think to herself. *I just remembered that I have a son.*

How do I know this? It's because they never call on a Friday night. They never, never call from nine to five. They never sit down and write a letter. It is just here and there during their occasional free time. So, during the workday I can answer the phone but, between seven and nine on weekend mornings I have to let the machine get it. I couldn't bear to actually talk to one of them. The casual indifference would shatter me. I can't take one more act of unlove.

I was listening to the radio the other day and heard a special report about the history of COINTELPRO. This was the counter-intelligence program maintained by the FBI in which they infiltrated every group of hopeful people on earth and confused them until they self-destructed and died. The WBAI announcer said that the agency's harassment of Marcus Garvey began in 1919. He said that the name of the FBI agent in charge of Garvey's demise was J. Edgar Hoover. In 1919. That's when I realized that my parents were trying to kill me. In fact, my entire family is in on it. Their plan is to invite me in and throw me out. Invite me in and throw me out, invite me in and throw me out until I have gone completely insane and hang myself in my own bedroom. It is their only possible motive.

Here's one of their favorite tactics for driving me insane. My mother likes to call me up and leave messages about obscure elderly relatives who have died, asking me to attend their funerals. She usually calls after we haven't seen each other for a year or two, asking me to show up at a gathering of relatives knowing that it would be the site of our first reunion. Does that sound appropriate? Does that sound like someone who really wants to see me?

My father's favorite tactic for killing me is to never call. The last time we spoke he made me cry. I said, "Dad, I just want you to be nice to me."

"You don't want us to be nice to you," he said. "You just want to blame us for your shortcomings."

Then he hung up the phone. My father hung up on me and never called me back. That was a year ago. He must be so relieved. Occasionally my parents go on vacation and I'll get a postcard signed MOM. Or a birthday card signed MOM. He's killing me, my dad. He obviously wants me to die.

Once I realized what was going on I started an in-depth investigation into my parents' death-squad tactics and strategies. That's when I understood, for the first time, how skillfully my brother and sister got recruited. It was a cold winter's Sunday back in 1968. I was ten. My sister was seven and my baby brother was three. My father had rented a car for a drive in the country but it was late afternoon and we still hadn't reached our goal. Instead, we drove around and around little country roads surrounded by snowy treetops and bushes of ice.

As a child I was always being gender-corrected. I was one of those little boys with a high squeaky voice who waved his hands in the air and got too excited. It made my parents deeply uncomfortable. They tried every way they could think of to convey their disapproval of my basic self, starting at the age of four. There was always an invisible Dave, one that had never existed and never could exist, that they expected to find, miraculously each morning at the breakfast table. And when, instead, all they got was little silly-willy me, with limp wrists and a will of steel, little courageous sissy-wissy me, they were deeply angry.

My father and mother and I got into an argument. Something about logic, the beauty of old-fashiondom, the fun of getting lost. I think those were my stated positions. My father, so upset that he wasn't being worshiped, finally stopped the car by the side of the road and ordered me out into the snow. All of this because I wouldn't keep from saying what I thought. I stood by the asphalt, just a little boy, as my father pulled away. But he didn't get far. After crawling about twenty feet ahead, the car stopped with the motor running. Some anonymous hand threw open the back door. The car sat, humming in the winter's stillness as its faceless inhabitants waited for me to approach, reproached.

His plan was so obvious. It called for me to be instantaneously shocked into submission by the fear of abandonment. I was supposed to panic and then cry, running towards my parents with gratitude and desire. He expected to dislodge me from my temporary manhood, reduced to a helpless child again. Finally, I was to rush towards the open door and reenter the car, humiliated, submissive and, most importantly, quiet.

But something else happened instead. I started walking away from the car, in the opposite direction on this one-way street. I didn't have to look behind me. They had obviously not moved. I kept walking, soberly, with determination instead of any frivolous vengeful emotion. And, finally, after turning the bend, I heard my father's car frantically pull away, knowing he would now have to negotiate incomprehensible country byways in order to be able to reapproach me in my fashion. A certain period of time passed, long enough for me to get lost in a reverie of understanding, until he finally found his way back along the same route from the beginning and was able to pick me up from the side of the road.

I don't know what I had imagined I would find inside that car. If I'd had to guess, I would have pictured the four of them rationally dissecting the map, trying to efficiently reach their goal, which was me. But, surprisingly, when I plopped back into the seat I was greeted instead by my sister and brother crying uncontrollably, with expressions of sheer terror on their two little faces. What had happened to me was the worst thing either of them could ever imagine. Their fear of my experience was to have a much more profound effect on their lives than the experience they dreaded had actually had on mine. This was the most important day in the lives of my brother and my sister. It was the day they learned fear, the day they were recruited to learn how to kill.

CHAPTER SEVENTEEN

WE LIVED IN A TWO-BEDROOM APARTMENT. MY sister, brother and me in one room and my parents in the other. They were looking for a larger place. My mother worked at a social service agency and my father was still in law school. I was a constant source of tension. I was not the way they had intended for me to be. This was increasingly obvious. But I was also undiscussable. My sister, on the other hand, had perfected her role as head snitch. The end result being that I was often in a place of fierce punishment including parental tantrums, spankings and, finally, banishment to the hallway of our apartment building.

When I imagine myself as a young boy it is a selection of images of privacy. Alone by the side of the road. Alone in the bathroom. Alone at the base of the family closet. And most casually, alone, sitting on the floor of the hallway outside the closed door of my parents' apartment. Sitting quietly as the neighbors came home from work.

"Are you locked out?" Grace from next door asked quietly.

"No," I said. "I'm being punished."

By this point the humiliation was gone. I had survived basic training and was now a full-time warrior. I informed neighbors of my punishment with complete nonchalance. It meant nothing to me. I took my blows, survived my trial by fire. And now, even punishment couldn't stop me. Nothing would make *me* ashamed.

For thirty-four years, which will soon be the totality of my life on earth, my family has been trying to kill me. Each one of them has their own personal motive for plotting my death.

My father's pathetic excuse was revealed only last summer as we sat sweating in his office. I had asked for an appointment and he scheduled me in between his 10:15 and his 11:05. Of course I was twenty-five minutes early. Since his entire emotional life travels in segments of forty-five minutes, mine, behavioristically, does the same. His first client had canceled so I approached that place only to find him standing anxiously in the doorway. Without clients to engage with, the poor guy had nothing to do.

"You blame me for everything," he said. "But it all actually has to do with you. You have always been a difficult child. You would never cooperate. Why, I remember when you were just born. Your mother loved you so much. She could never have imagined that you would grow up into this."

He leaned back into his chair and buried his chin into his neck.

"I would come home from the hospital and you would be lying in your crib, crying and crying. You must have been three months old. You were so agitated. Something was troubling you even then. There I was, a young law student, and I patted you on the back but you wouldn't be comforted. You've been a problem ever since."

My mother's complaints are a bit more complex.

"We were always so close," she has said. "Maybe you don't remember this but you told me everything."

I have flashed this sentence through my mind a thousand times. I do remember my mother standing up for me in a conflict with another child in grade school. Johnny Goodman. Fuck him. I was about seven and making what was then known as "phony phone calls." I dialed whatever numbers popped into my head and said things like "Hey Mack, we know you've got the jewels. Bring them over to Ninth Street or you're a goner."

Things like that.

Unfortunately, one of the numbers that popped into my mind was not as arbitrary as I might have wished, but rather belonged to Johnny. His mother had the bad judgment to press charges by calling my mother and informing her that I had anonymously threatened Mrs. Goodman's life. Technically, this was true, but in terms of intention, culpability and context, it was utterly false. Of course, being prepubescent and having not yet read any great books, I was unable to fully explain the extenuating circumstances and so was forced, through lack of resources, to deny the crime.

My mother promptly got on the phone with Mrs. Goodman and defended my honor. I think that somewhere it was obvious to her that Mrs. Goodman's precision of accusation was virtually impossible to match with my psychic state — with what kind of person I have always been. And armed with this correct hunk of instinctual information, for the first and final time she did the right thing. She defended me.

Unfortunately, after she hung up the phone with Mrs. Goodman, I fled, crying into the bottom of our closet and sat there shaking with grief. I did not know how to articulate the truth but could not live with a distortion. It was not an issue of honesty but rather that the real truth was acceptable to me and I wanted it to be acceptable to her. So, unable to survive with either option, I confessed to my mother that I had indeed committed the crime as defined by Mrs. Goodman's language, even though it was unrecognizable in comparison with the actual event. My mother never defended me again.

CHAPTER EIGHTEEN

L AST MONDAY NIGHT IN THE RESTAURANT THERE
was an unexpected discomfort. I walked in with
Fabio, Robert's new Italian boyfriend and there was Kurt,
suddenly, with some ugly short white man who could not be
his lover. They were standing ahead of us on line waiting for a
table. I said hello, awkwardly, and remembered suddenly how
much taller he is. His hair is shaved at the base but has a
crown of hanging dreds that fall gamely on his neck, like a
black version of Veronica Lake. Suddenly he was so much
taller than me that eye level was directly into his razor burn.

As always he was cool, very poised and dignified. I managed to listen to Fabio's yapping politely without ever once
turning to look at Kurt's lithe back. But finally I did have to
pass by on the way to the urinals and managed to touch him
gently, but possessively, on the shoulder. It was a natural,
open touch designed expressly to feel the shape of his slender
back. I waited in the stall for him to follow, hoping we could
fuck on the stairs, but he never came around.

At home that night I played a Minnie Ripperton album a
couple of times. What a star. If she had been called to opera
instead of to schlock she would have been a coloratura—that
firm, thin, high soprano. More dear.

Minnie reminds me of the threat of impending banality that I have to live with daily. I see it creeping everywhere. How to keep jazz from becoming dinner music. How to keep love poems off of greeting cards. How to keep AIDS from being pathetic.

I read in Herve Guilbert's book that Foucault died, not knowing exactly what had hit him. His lover found his hand-cuffs and whips and couches full of leftover manuscripts on such trifles as the history of socialism. Charles Ludlam was the most profound loss. America doesn't even know what she's missing. I saw him and his lover Everett in *Irma Vep* and sat sobbing at his funeral. It was the first time I cried after my boyfriend's death in '82. But what do we do with all the medi-ocrities who never created anything worth remembering and never would have even if they had lived to be eighty-five? It drives me crazy how quickly the great ones get canonized. *Blah-blah-blah is such a terrible loss.* Does that mean that the death of one mediocre slob is not as terrible? Do fags have to be geniuses to justify living?

There is almost nothing left to be said about my dead boyfriend Don at this late date. We'd only been going out for a few months before he suddenly called me from the hospital. I'd never been in one before, not since I was born. It was so unbelievable. Most of my memories of Don are in bed, plastic tubes up his nose and arms, lying there, infusing. Where the fuck were his parents? Why did they abandon us?

I remember one afternoon I was sitting next to his bed. He was lying there, wan, very anxious, plastic in his orifices. I looked down at the pillow and he looked up at me and waved his eyes in one of those high camp queenie gestures that means completely giving up and saying *fuck you* to the world at the same time. It was so absurd. I still don't believe it.

For a while I tried really hard to remember his chest the way it was at first in my hands. Like the side of a mountain. But the real memory is tired and sad with silvery worms of plastic coming out of his nose. That is how I will always picture my love.

By 2:00 A.M. I was going through my phone book wondering who I could possibly call. Could I call Kurt? It really was too late. What about all those people in San Francisco? Amy is in Berlin. Bob isn't agitated enough for late night phone calls. John is dead. Mark is dead. Sam is dead. The other Bob is waiting for his boyfriend to die. Maybe I'll call Kurt. I called Bob.

"Hi Bob, how's kicks?"

"Oh, Fred seems to be doing a lot better."

"That's great," I said.

"Yeah, today he went outside on his own."

"How are you doing?"

"Fine. Let's see. This morning I took Fred to the herbalist. Those Chinese herbs are really miracle drugs. Then I took him into the clinic for a spinal tap and it really made him feel a lot better. He's not so disoriented as he was last week."

"Great. How are *you* doing?"

"Fine. Tomorrow I'm taking Fred to a neurologist and we're doing exercises every day."

"Do you get out at all?"

"Oh yeah, I get out. We have plenty of friends who come by. Thursday I take Fred to massage and we've been trying this vitamin B for neuropathy. Assotto Saint recommended it. It coats your nerve endings apparently."

"Whatever."

"Ooops, gotta go. Fred needs to eat. Thanks for calling."

"Bye Bob."

But he had already hung up.

Then I called Kurt, let the phone ring three times and hung up. I never leave messages. I know they're there screening the calls, staring at the machine as the little cassette tape clicks into place. I do it too. If they don't pick up they don't want to talk and then if you leave a message you're at their mercy. I could call Jose in Phoenix. He'll remember me. But what would we talk about? If I wanted phone sex I'd dial 1-900. I could call David in LA but he'll think something's up and ask me four thousand times if I'm all right. Joe is dead. I could call Linda except she's so annoying. Phil Zwickler is dead. Bo Houston is dead. John Bernd is dead. Martin Worman is dead. Jon Greenberg is dead. Robert Garcia is dead. I already talked to Carl last week. Don is dead. Would Don and I be boyfriends now if he was still alive? Would he be taking care of me?

CHAPTER NINETEEN

I'M SICK OF TALKING TO GAY MEN AND LESBIANS ABOUT AIDS. I don't want to share one more word. When I talk to a straight person there is my pain and then they can be the sympathetic observer. But with other gay people it just brings out everything they're living with too. Then both of us descend into a frenzy of pain and don't have any way out. It is like two magnificent lions with nothing to talk over but their cage. I'd rather describe it to some straight person who's never been there and really wants to know all the details.

Don's deathbed scene was too huge to be cinematic. If there was a new art form combining nature, opera and war, that might be sufficient. I'd been sitting by the bed for days and decided, that morning, to go out for a walk. I don't know why. But I put on my overcoat and stepped outside the hospital. New York University Medical Center. Dying young men and Orthodox Jews. Only the best. Co-op Care at NYU was like staying at the Marriott. When the *rebbetizins* had chemo you couldn't tell the difference. What hair?

I went outside and thought about buying a pack of cigarettes. I don't smoke but it was in defiance of all those homosexual pulmonary lesions and Jews on iron lungs. On the way back from the store I passed this old drag queen, trying to find enough change to get on the bus. Her look was Fourteenth Street Puerto Rican bleached-blond toothless junkie. You know those queens all work their chosen looks to perfection. She could hardly count her change. Then, as soon as the bus pulled away, I saw another out-of-place queen. She looked like she was coming back from the night before, lost her wig and just had too much white face makeup from the forehead down. She was hiding her head behind an umbrella even though it wasn't raining. My people, in such states of decline.

I came back to the hospital and went, as always, to take a look at Don. He opened his eyes and said, "Call my family."

Of course now it is old news, that when a PWA says to call his family he is just about to die. At that time I didn't yet know the ropes but fortunately followed my instincts and called.

"Come now," I said. "Come right now."

His sisters only had to fly in from Philadelphia but they made it about five hours later and came bustling into the hospital room. Now Donny was covered in KS—I mean really covered. And he was toothpick thin. You didn't even want to touch him because you thought for sure he'd break. So what did his sisters say when they came into the hospital room?

"You look good," they said.

Shocked, they stayed and chatted for about fifteen minutes and then announced that they were going to go over to their uncle's house to drop off their stuff and would come back early the next morning. And then they left. I guess they didn't know that he was dying.

Afterwards I sat with him all night until the morning when the doctor offered Don the morphine drip.

"Do you want the drip, Donny?" I asked quietly. "Or do you want to stay a little longer?"

"I want to stay a little longer," he said.

Those were his last words.

Of course nowadays there is a new technology. The most recent death that I attended was sealed by a little patch that the doctor, unofficially, gave us to place on Ross's chest. After whatever it was went through his skin and he died, we just removed it and threw it away. No one ever had to know.

About twenty minutes after Don died, I stepped out into the hallway to look for a doctor. I saw this guy Manuel, also looking for a doctor. His friend had just died too. Later that day we decided to go coffin hunting together. He took me to this showroom on the Upper West Side where the coffins were laid out like new cars. Manuel was older and had already done this a few times and he knew the salesman pretty well. I was very impressed at the way Manuel resisted all the guilt-tripping they try to do to you. They tried to sell you coffins that were waterproof, or that had velvet interiors just because they know you feel guilty for being alive. But Manuel made sure I bought the cheapest one.

Later on in the week I called him when I realized that Don's burial would cost almost $15,000.

"It's your responsibility," he said. "If you ask the family for help you'll never forgive yourself."

And now I know that he was right. Paying for your lover's funeral is the gay version of a bar mitzvah. It is how you know that you have become a man.

CHAPTER TWENTY

I T IS REALLY HARD TO BE ANGRY AT YOUR PARENTS IF they didn't rape you or burn you in boiling oil. Thanks to twelve-step programs the parental discourse is at such a high pitch that if they didn't sell you into white slavery it would be hard to get a compassionate response out of your friends. That old boring, middle-class despisal of gaydom is just so common.

"Get over it," my friends say on the twenty-seventh cocktail.

I was talking to Manuel about this the other night. He's the one I finally called at 3:00 A.M. He was up late thinking about Dostoyevski per usual.

"One thing my mother always told me," Manuel said. "You'll meet people in your life whose beliefs you despise but they'll be really nice. And then there will be people whose beliefs you embrace but they're awful."

"Therefore . . . ?"

"Well, Dostoyevski," Manuel said. "He believed in God and Mother Russia. So, reactionary, yet the characters are marvelous."

Manuel was a famous poet in Cuba but since he's been living here it might as well be Atlantis. So, he punishes himself for obscurity by wearing striped shirts and plaid jackets, going to twelve-step programs and giving up on sex.

"I was gay in Cuba but it was strange. I was out, living with my lover but we were bizarre. I felt too alone."

"What about other gay people?"

"They're there. The apartments are so small. You'll have some minister or Communist Party functionary living in the same house with her son and his lover. It requires a lot of coping. A lot of silence and a lot of eye contact."

"Manuel, I don't understand why you gave up on sex. Don't you think about dick day and night?"

"Yes," he said. "But the average American penis is five inches, unfortunately. So . . ."

"You mean Cuban dick is bigger?"

"No. Smaller. But so much more succulent."

Don had a beautiful dick. I think. I can't remember. He was a real hero. I watched him going off to teach classes in the morning, his face covered with lesions. He went into the hospital the last time on Valentine's Day and rotted there until Memorial Day. When he was dying his body was covered in those lesions. He asked me to massage his shoulders and I did the first time but then I said that I couldn't do it anymore. He said, "All right."

His anus was a big, black cancerous hole. It was monstrous. When he was dying I dreamed I worked as a busboy in a coffee shop. I earned fifty dollars and stood on line with my bill to buy coffee. A man came over and started to take my money. A policeman saw him but didn't do anything about it.

"Why didn't you help me?" I asked the policeman.

"He might have had a gun," he said.

When Don first started to get sick we barely knew each

other. He asked me to make sure that if it ever got critical I wouldn't let him be reduced to infancy. That I would put him out of his pain. But then the time came and it was too late. I realized too late what was involved. I couldn't take Donny's life. He had to do it. If he didn't want to end up in diapers then he had to choose death before he was too weak to make that choice. He couldn't leave that up to me. What did I know about death? I was only twenty-four. Now I know more than there is to know. If I ever started mourning I'd be mourning all my days. The tears would never stop.

One night I got blown at Sperm Bank and was coming home late, kind of staggering after five or six beers. There was Manuel, standing on the street corner buying the next day's *New York Times*. He was illuminated, in his clown suit, under the bare streetlight and all around him the sidewalk was covered in litter. It was a carpet of junk.

"David," he said in that booming oak voice, his pudgy face flat against a bad haircut and a large earring badly placed in his soft earlobe.

"Manuel, I was just thinking about Donny."

I didn't even know that I was thinking about Donny. Something had flashed into the back of my mind when I was having sex. Some kind of shape.

"What about him?"

"Why did he have to die?"

Manuel folded the *Times* under his arm and shoved his hands into his pocket.

"Have to?"

"But he died for no reason and no one would help me."

"I know," Manuel said.

"But Donny, Don, Don, Don . . . Don . . . Don . . . Don, Don, Don."

"Shut up," he said. "Stop talking about Don. Every time I see you that's all you have to say. Life is short now. Time has a different meaning. Don has been dead for a millennium. His name should be invoked once a year at a religious ritual and then conveniently forgotten, for my sake if no one else's."

"But, Don."

"Shut up," he said. "Or never talk to me again."

"There's Kurt," I said and we both looked across the street. What a specimen. He wore sparkling white jeans pulled high around the waist and a loose white shirt in which he shone like the goddess of masculine beauty. Like Sir Venus.

"Who's that?" Manuel asked, getting sidetracked by a twenty-four-hour newsstand with a better selection than the one we'd left behind.

"If that man would fuck me I would live," I said.

"Look," Manuel said gleefully. "They have all the new gay magazines here. They have *Fags and Fag Hags*. They have *CQ.*"

"What's that stand for?"

"Control Queens."

"Don't you ever read pornography?" I asked, exasperated.

"Of course," Manuel said. "I read it day and night."

CHAPTER TWENTY-ONE

I STILL GO TO ACT UP EVERY WEEK. I NEVER DO ANY-thing. I rarely go to demonstrations and I have never belonged to a committee. I used to sleep with this guy from Needle Exchange but when he found out I was positive he wouldn't even talk to me. Now he's got a big shot PWA boyfriend from Treatment and Data Committee and wears him on his arm like a sign of liberal pride. But when our eyes meet he always looks away.

Basically I go to ACT UP for the floor show. I bring my Walkman and a couple of magazines for the boring parts but when it is really cooking I love the drama. It is the true story of *One Life to Live.* One of the regular elements of the ACT UP saga is that there is always some wildly talented, articulate, dying one who is everyone's emotional and spiritual leader for a few months until he actually does die. Then a new one emerges from the ashes. For example, my hero one year was Bob Rafsky. He was a former closeted advertising executive who said the most amazing things at just the right occasions. I loved him because his passion was so out front.

Here is an example of Bob's legendary greatness. When Charlie died in July after thirty hospitalizations in two years, the family organized the memorial service. It was one of those situations where the family was really okay and really loved him so everyone kind of stepped back and let them deal with it and then, of course, they fucked up the whole thing. The family were some kind of upper-class Unitarians and they constructed a starched white-collar funeral complete with excerpts from Benjamin Britten and readings of poems with the word "Byzantium" in them. They even produced the requisite nerdy ex-boyfriend who stood up there earnestly and then made matters worse by singing a Joni Mitchell song.

The Charlie that was sexy and a dancer and angry because men shunned him when they knew his diagnosis, was nowhere to be seen in this service. Some dyke stood up and said that in his will he'd donated his computer and printer to the Lesbian Herstory Archives. But that was about as gay as it got. Finally, at the end they invited anyone in the room to get up and speak. This was followed by a barrage of straight girls who had known him from prep school. All just *sooo* emotional over his death, unlike the war-weary ACT UPers seething in the pews.

Each girl came up in her flowered dress and sang some stupid song or broke down into tears about Charlie being gone. All I could think of was *Where the hell were you, asshole? I never saw you at any demonstration. I never saw you trying to get the price of Foscarnet reduced as Charlie was going blind.* I felt like those girls were killing me. Just killing me. I looked around and caught Walter's eye. He was crying out of frustration and being overwhelmed, not something so bourgeois as grief. That's reserved for straight people on their fourth or fifth death. Grief doesn't exist for us.

Right then, Rafsky got up. He was covered in Kaposi's from head to toe and had taken to wearing tiny cut-off jean shorts and spaghetti strap T-shirts so that every person he passed on the subway would have to deal with it. As he walked up to the platform, Walter and I smiled at each other like Victoria's messenger finally did come riding.

"The least we can do," Bob said carefully into the microphone, "is not take false comfort."

And then he sat down. It was so beautiful. He told them that they were not even doing the minimum. Then we all retired downstairs for cookies and iced tea.

There's something beautiful about the way Bob showed his pain at ACT UP meetings. He's dead now, but then it just reinforced how we are really a family. That we, the couple of hundred people who are still alive and still willing to come together in that room every Monday night after five years. We are so intimate that we can act out all of our pain in front of each other. We can tell each other the truth.

One night Andrew Barton was forced to come to a meeting to explain why he, as our community representative, had voted against allowing the community to attend meetings of some government committee. The dykes and some guys were really appalled and a few had the balls to say so. But that's the thing about Andrew. He's a real bastard but he always acts like if some miracle cure around the corner is ever going to be found, he's the one who is going to find out about it first. So, he might know how to keep us alive. That's why we've all got to stay on his good side. All of us who are infected feel that way. It's that Daddy thing. We still hope that some male is going to come along and make it all better. But real daddy never did that so why the hell should Prince Andrew?

Anyway, he was going on and on in his usual arrogant, snobby way using all kinds of scientific terms that he knew for a fact none of us could understand. That was the whole point of his speech, of course. To prove, for the thousandth time that he really can understand things that we can't understand and so there is no way that we, the non-understanders, have any right to make him *accountable*. He went on and on and people started to get really pissed off.

Finally, Rick, a mild-mannered architect, dared to challenge even one point and Andrew grabbed the microphone like it was someone else's big dick and shouted into it that he wasn't going to put up with this kind of behavior. Then he stormed out, followed by a coterie of dying men, each hoping that Andrew's interrupted, unfinished sentence contained the key to their survival.

Those of us there primarily for dramatic reasons followed them out into the hall, while Bob Rafsky stood there and bellowed at the top of his fatherly lungs.

"Andrew Barton is the only person in this room who can save my life."

Later that night I saw some dyke go up to Bob and look him straight in the eye. She said, "Bob, I wish that you did not have AIDS. But I do not believe that Andrew Barton is going to save your life. And he might ruin this organization."

I didn't hear his answer but that dyke's statement just froze me. How dare she speak to him that way. How dare anyone tell anyone else that they are going to die. It's like a family, I'm telling you. Everyone is too far out of line right in front of each other. I never bring friends to ACT UP. It's like bringing a friend home to dinner when your family is *Who's Afraid of Virginia Woolf?*

CHAPTER TWENTY-TWO

I STARTED MENTIONING AIDS TO MY PARENTS AROUND the time that Don got sick. I waited to see how they would respond. When they didn't respond, I couldn't say anymore. I just mentioned. Mentioned, mentioned, mentioned, mentioned. By 1985 I was mentioning it every time I saw them. I started repeating names of different young men, saying what hospital they were in, that I had gone to visit this one and that one and how they were doing. I'd say their names over again.

"I just came from visiting my friend Robert at NYU. You remember Robert? He's the one I mentioned last time who is in Co-op Care? Remember, I mentioned that he was trying out this new drug that was really promising? Well, I gotta go now. I've got to go over to visit Robert and bring him some vitamins. I'll let you know how he's doing next time."

But the next time I'd wait and wait. I'd wade through all the stories of eighty-year-olds with heart attacks and whose daughter was getting married and I'd wait and wait for one word. I just wanted them to utter that word. That word was *Robert.*

"Remember my friend Robert? Robert? Remember I mentioned him to you last time? He's the one who is in NYU

Medical Center. You remember Robert. Robert? That's the one. Right?"

I'd come to seders straight from funerals and have to sit there wrenched with anger and pain as my parents would go on and on about their stupid opinions about this city policy and that city policy and who got fired and hired and whose daughter's husband got his whatever degree.

I went out to San Francisco to spend two months living with Paul, sitting around with him in the house watching Geraldo Rivera from his bed until he was too weak to hold the remote. I called my parents before I went and told them four times I was going to stay with Paul. Paul, Paul, Paul, Paul, Paul. I wanted them to call me. I cried at night on the mattress on the floor. But they wouldn't call me and say that one word. Paul.

My brother came out there on business with his girl-friend but could never find the time to come by the house to meet Paul. Finally, I had to go way over to the other side of town, the straight side, where he was staying and we went out for dinner. He never asked about Paul. Never mentioned it. He just went on and on about his business connections. Finally I started saying something about what it is like to live with a dying thirty-two-year-old. But my brother didn't . . . never brought it up.

The boundaries of parental love are so narrow.

My parents have always hated me for being gay. They've always wished I would disappear, but nothing has ever made me so nauseous and vicious as the gulf that AIDS has created between me and them. I came from Beekman visiting Saul with lesions on his lungs to a family dinner for my sister's birthday. She was feeling down because her seventy-year-old graduate school professor had just died and my mother turned to her and said, "You've had more people die in your life than anyone I know."

I froze, bread halfway to my mouth. My mother caught me as though I had committed the crime.

"You mean the AIDS thing," she said. "You're always looking for ammunition against us."

And these reactions are so typical. My friends and I exchange them like baseball cards. This is how America treats us. It's not AIDS that makes them hate us. They hated us before because they could not control us. They could not make us be just like them. Now, they're glad we're dying. They're uncomfortable about how they feel but really they're relieved. There's nothing on earth that could kill us more efficiently than parental indifference.

CHAPTER TWENTY-THREE

MANUEL CALLED ME TOO EARLY ON A GRAY SUN-DAY to go see Gregg Araki's film, *The Living End*. I'd missed it the first time around and now some gay film festival stuck with last year's hits was playing it again—one time only. I knew that it was about two HIV-positive guys so I got there an hour early worrying it would be sold out. Of course, every New Yorker would race to the theater to see a movie about two HIV-positive guys. What else would they have to talk about? But the house was half full and Manuel came staggering in only five minutes before showtime, soaked through to the skin because he's too unconscious to ever bring an umbrella.

I was a bit peeved, besides, when it became apparent that he had also invited Tom and Lyle to come along too because I know that they are HIV-positive.

What a fun way to spend the weekend, I thought. *Oh, YAY!*

Tom and Lyle brought some dyke along to round out the whole scenario. We looked like an ad for National Brotherhood Week. Lyle and I were the only ones in our little crowd that resembled the rest of the guys in the audience. Clean-shaven little white guys. One big living Gap ad.

Araki's film was about two cute boys who fall in love and have HIV. The stud has decided that HIV made him free—so now he can ride around America having sex and beating people up, killing them and not worry about a thing. He won't have a real life anymore. He'll only have a glamorous one. The other guy, equally sexy but too skinny, goes along with it because he wants to get laid, and somewhere in the back of his mind he thinks *this might be the way out.* Of course the inevitable rub is that instead of being freed by HIV, Stud's whole life is now entirely run by HIV because he can't let himself live normally again. And, ultimately, that's what we diseased pariahs want more than anything else on earth—NORMALCY.

The final message of the movie is that you can't get out from under the grip of HIV. You can't do anything about it. That's the thing we all now know about AIDS. You have to accept it.

But there was one really beautiful moment that ran through my mind repeatedly as we all stepped out of the theater in that predictable, boring silence. I was thinking about how wonderful it would be to have a boyfriend to love me and hold me and we could have cinematic HIV together and die happily ever after. That's romance.

"Cocktails or coffee?" the dyke said and we all screamed, "Cocktails."

What followed was a maniacally singleminded journey to find a place with food and drink that we could afford and so, after dismissing a number of tasteless, overpriced *endroits* for heterosexuals, we returned to the dyke-owned Pharmacy on Avenue A and Ninth Street, which was as bourgeois as any of us ever really got unless someone else was picking up the tab.

We ordered our eggs Benedict, Bloody Marys, et cetera, et cetera. Then Manuel starts rambling on and on about something about AIDS but, of course, only in the abstract. The three of us squeezed our limes and looked at the tablecloth and at the saltshaker.

"I just finally read *And the Band Played On*," Manuel starts blathering. "I avoided it for years because of its horrible reputation."

Then he starts in with this statistic and that one. Reciting all these tired theories. I really wanted to scream at this point. That's all guys ever talk about: DDI, DDC, DDI, DDC.

Or else it's Morgue Geography: *"Did you hear that Gary died just six days after his lover Danny?"*

"But I thought Danny died in June."

"No, that was Danny Schapiro that died a month ago, this is Danny Rich who died last week. Then Steve died ahead of schedule."

"Again? I thought he died last month."

"That was Steven. This is Steve."

Follow the bouncing corpse.

Anyway, Manuel kept up his verbal stupor but Tom and Lyle and I didn't say a word. Finally we all started talking about how the film was shot and what kind of lens he had blah, blah, blah. Conveniently it reminded Manuel of a Joan Crawford movie, at last. So we got into that and ordered a second round of Marys.

"When I was a kid," the dyke says, "I used to listen to Jimi Hendrix and think he was saying *'Scuse me while I kiss this guy.* So I thought he was gay. When the radio played *'And the wind cried Mary,'* I knew it was true."

That broke the ice. So, without missing a beat she said, "How did you feel about the movie, personally?"

Are all dykes born social workers or what? They've got this delivery that lets you say what you want to say but it is so fucking perfect it is annoying. It is devastating. Still Tom heroically tried to resist by speaking instead as an African-American and not as a diseased pariah.

"Well, I was really troubled by his insistence on using an all-white cast. He is Japanese, after all."

"His parents were in internment camps," she said.

Just the kind of facts dykes keep at their fingertips.

"It bothered me that he had to pretend that the world is white," Tom replied.

"No," she said, not to be disobeyed. "I mean, how did you feel about what he was saying about HIV?"

Immediately a very jumpy conversation ensued between Tom and me and Lyle about how much we hated those pretty guys who played the leads. And how much we hated the ro-manticism. We really got going but even that couldn't thaw poor Manuel. He kept looking at his plate and making com-ments about the hollandaise sauce being rotten. I felt sorry for that schmuck. He was surrounded by the faces of his fu-ture ghosts.

"Those guys were too spoiled," Lyle said on Mary num-ber three.

"Spoiled?"

That was the dyke talking again. They like to repeat your words back to you to show that they're listening.

"Yeah, guys like that pretend that they're tough. They *home boys*. They *rebels who ain't got no cause*. But when it comes down to it they'll never do anything really bad unless it's with their dicks. That's why we can't get anywhere with this fuck-ing disease. Gay boys are too well behaved. Chelsea is never going to go up in flames like South Central LA."

Lyle was the white one but he dipped occasionally into

overdone black slang. Tom, the black one, never did it in front of me.

"What do you mean *spoiled*?" I asked.

"Well," he said. "You know how they had these stolen credit cards in the movie and could therefore go anywhere and do anything?"

"Yeah?"

"Well, is that really as far as a fag can imagine when it comes to disorderly conduct? When we're bad we don't rob banks. We go to banks."

"Yeah," said Tom. "In real life we don't have that credit card. So what are *we* supposed to do?"

CHAPTER TWENTY-FOUR

T HE LAST TIME I SAW MY PARENTS WAS MOTHER'S Day. I had just come from relieving the guy in Gino's care group and walked into the apartment just in time to find that Gino had shit all over himself.

"I just came from Gino's apartment," I said to my parents as we sat around the kitchen table drinking mimosas.

"Gino shit all over himself and the other guy didn't know what to do. He was so busy retching every time he got near the bed that he'd let Gino lie in his own shit for almost half an hour trying to get up the guts to deal with it."

"I've been through this twice before," I said casually to my disgusted parents as I speared a canned asparagus. "Of course."

I crossed my legs like a nelly Gene Kelly.

"So, I ran the tub and then lifted Gino up into it. Washed him off. Washed myself off. Threw out the sheets and remade the bed. Then I went home and changed and then I came over here."

"Well, I saw a client, just the other day, with cancer," my father said. "A fifty-year-old man. We see this every day."

"More and more people come into our agency needing home care," my mother added.

That's when I started crying and screaming. My parents

hate it when I cry and scream because I am a grown man and not supposed to ever act that way. To them it is a sign of how wrong and bad I am. What a bad seed I am. How disturbed.

"What do you want from us?" my mother shouted. "I don't even know the man."

"Do you want to meet him?" I asked, pathetically.

And for that moment, like a thousand moments before, I suddenly flashed, foolishly, that my dream would come true. I flashed that my father and mother would come with me to visit Gino and would ask him how he felt. They would ask me questions about myself too. They would come to a gay play and read a gay book and call me up in the morning when there was something vile on the television because *they have a gay child*. And no one is going to hurt their gay child as long as they still have air in their lungs. Because they love their gay son and all parents must love their gay children. From their first faggy moment until they're taken off of life supports, all parents must love their gay children. They must not treat us like this.

My sister started in on a story about some student of hers with a terminal disease and something she saw on TV. My brother was pacing back and forth making business calls on the telephone and not participating in the conversation at all. Then my sister started talking about her trip to LA.

I've seen so many people die and where the fuck were their families? Our families want us to be destroyed. They sit around talking about the toaster-oven while we are doomed and they don't even mention it. David Wojnarowicz's brother flew in after he had died in order to attend the memorial service. The family "thanked" his lover for taking care of him. Who are they to "thank" us? We are the real family. They are just a bunch of cold-hearted killers.

"You complain about me, but it could be a lot worse," my father told me during those twenty-five minutes of precious attention I received, that day, in his office. "Some parents don't even speak to their homosexual children," he said. "Some parents won't even let them in the house."

A man's enemies will be those in his own household.
—MATTHEW 10

The night after my breakdown, my brother left a message on my phone machine.

"Dave, this is your brother. I'm sick of this bullshit. You fucking asshole. Fuck off."

They're so unaware that we are suffering. They've got it all wrong. They think we're pretending and mentioning it repeatedly just to ruin their day. Just to guilt trip them for something they didn't do. How could we do this to them?

Then I took a look in the mirror.

This property is condemned, I thought.

That was the first night I had the sweats.

CHAPTER TWENTY-FIVE

L AST NIGHT WAS A BEAUTIFUL NIGHT. YESTERDAY WAS a beautiful day. Rita called me up out of the blue to go over to Tompkins Square Park because the city had finally reopened it and everyone in the neighborhood was walking around taking their first look.

"God, it's beautiful," I said.

And it was.

New paths, new drinking fountains that worked, new benches, new chess tables for old men. A dog run, bike paths, three playgrounds and a basketball court.

"No rats," Rita noticed right away.

First we walked around oohing and aahing about how peaceful and lovely everything was and then we started noticing past the surface, analyzing the situation. This process— from acceptance to critique—usually takes a New Yorker eight to ten minutes.

"Well, it's not like the three hundred homeless people who used to live in this park now have nice apartments," Rita said. "But the Parks Department did do a good job with the rodents."

"Out of sight, out of mind," I said, thinking of myself.

"I just came back from my first Lesbian Avenger meeting," she said.

"How did it go?"

"Great. I thought up the slogan for the new banner."

"What is it?"

"S.O.S.," Rita said. "Suck Our Sisters, Suck Our Selves."

The homeless were so gone. They were like anthropological relics. They were like me—exterminated. Mayans buried their dead with water and plates of food. Archaeologists discovered that the plates lasted longer than their bones. Here and there a fragmented skull and piece of spinal chord. The memento outlasts the memory, outlasts the dead, the living.

"Why are you crying?" she asked.

"It has to do with my parents," I said.

"What?"

"It's just that I want my mother to . . ." I was choked with tears.

"To be interested in you?" Rita asked, trying to be helpful.

"No," I said, really sobbing. "I wish that my mother . . ."

"You wish that she really wanted to know what you were doing?" she tried again.

"No," I said, trying desperately to get a grip. "I just wish that she really wanted to see me."

There were no drug addicts in the park at all, which I attributed to the clusters of policemen at every entrance. Just a few, very demure homeless were sitting in the sun trying not to be noticed. Other, more acceptable residents walked around slightly dazed. They couldn't believe that something so nice could actually be for them.

"Midnight curfew," Rita pointed out, reading the signs. "That's to make sure no one sleeps over."

"Too bad," I said. "The neighborhood is open until four in the morning. I guess we have to scamper back at twelve to our hot little apartments."

"I wonder if they killed the rats or just chased them into the stores across the street," Rita asked as we both sat down on a bench.

A monk in New York strode steadily across the park. A blond girl was reading Turgenev. A dyke came by dressed in black, her breasts under control. Two black men in white pants, two candles and a dog. That skinny guy had a red backpack. The couple next to us was starting to coo. The boy whistled the Mister Softee theme song. One young woman had a cane. Another skimmed *Allure*. There was a stunned silence. The park was so clean it was only a dream. The homeless were out of consciousness now. Then I remembered that, actually, they're living on our front stoops now, but the landlords live in Nyack. I wanted a cigarette. We were all dazed. I could see the aesthetic beauty of the world, and I do have the desire to live. But there is not enough anger for everything that makes me angry. And there is not enough grief for my grief. Learning this fact/insight/lesson/inauguration/design is so painful. Because now, at age thirty-four, getting tired, having had my first symptom, I really know what it is I'm going to miss out on.

"What's going on?" she asked.

"My foot hurts so much, I feel like my body weight is crushing it. I feel like it will never get better. My bones hurt. I can't breathe—there's too much pollution. My poor legs. Am I going to have to hobble like this from now on? I know you always bounce back for the first few years but maybe I'll be the exception. I'll go on tour of the Bahamas as *America's shortest-living survivor*. Last night I had the sweats again."

"What are they like?"

"Well," I said, trying to isolate it. "Right before I went to bed I felt really tired and sore. My bones hurt. And then in the middle of the night I woke up freezing and then totally sweating, my bones hurting and the sheets wet. Just like in all the books. At least they got that right."

"How about today?"

"No sweats at all since then."

"That's good," Rita said. "What a relief."

I would just rather that she told me that she didn't know what to say instead of searching around the universe for the one possible positive—the absence of pain at any given moment.

"Do you want to come to a party tonight?"

"Where?" I asked because I had been thinking about going to Eastside Sauna.

"In Brooklyn, in Dyke Slope. It's that girl Margaret. You know, she's a dark-skinned black girl, she works for the *New York Times*? Her lover is that blond thing Killer fucked last year."

"What's in it for me?" I asked.

"Some nice boys."

"Black ones?" I asked, just to annoy her.

"Seems like it, doesn't it? Or were you thinking about going to that sex club for HIV-positives only?"

Eternity is a hooded skeleton, a human tiger with a butterfly on his scalp. A bespectacled burro waving a death's-head flag. Dried bread. A one-armed Inca with tattooed knees, his sister plays the mandolin with artificial fingernails. A uniformed pig holds his hand down a wood pile. The scarecrow is bleeding. My tongue is too big. There a swastika in red, white and blue. A bag of gold. A blank, open book.

"No, I wasn't," I said. It had never even occurred to me. Sex camp for the pariahs, please. "I'll come to the party early. Then I'm going to go out."

Immediately I started trying to decide what kind of pants to wear. Should I wear my sexy dick-outlined black jeans which will make my legs swell up like lead balloons—or should I wear those casual, drawstring African pants that all us swollen-legged HIV-positives wear to show how casual we are? Which one? Which one? Which one? Which one?

PART THREE

KILLER
IN LOVE

CHAPTER TWENTY-SIX

(IN WHICH KILLER ATTENDS
A MEMORIAL SERVICE.)

♡ ♡ ♡ ♡

Sunday afternoon Rita stopped by but I was still in bed with my new girlfriend Troy and had forgotten all about everything.

"How can you forget about a memorial service?" she asked. "Hey, I see you've got that new brand of glue trap."

"Sorry," I answered. "I didn't really forget. I just got vague."

We walked over to Fourteenth Street and the river for Robert Garcia's memorial service which was being held at Meat, where I guess he liked to fuck. I know the area because I have a plant account right down the street. Plus Meat turns into the Clit Club every Friday night. Not that I go there that much now that I'm a little older, but that street has the most used condoms and used streetwalkers per square foot than any other strip of cement west of the Atlantic Ocean—which makes it noticeable.

"God, I feel so weird, I haven't talked to David in weeks. He's the person I first met Robert through. Have you?"

"Yeah," Rita said. "You have to call three or four times to get a response."

"I guess he's in no mood to be the one to reach out."

"Whatever," Rita said. "I think he's going through that phase. You know, the envy of the dying for the living. If you're not the type who can brush it off, better not to talk at all."

"But what if we get in a fight?" I asked, panicking. Thinking again of my long lost parents. "And he dies?"

"He will definitely die," she said.

"I know," I answered, exasperated at Rita's bullheaded position. "But what if we have a fight and he dies and nothing was resolved?"

"Nothing is ever resolved," Rita said, tired. "That's one of those fake concepts. How can you resolve with a man dead at thirty-four? What kind of peace can you make with that? Lately I've been thinking that the conflict is for the best. Because then we are not pretending that anything about this can ever be reasonable."

Walking into the club in the middle of the day was kind of depressing since, like most dives, it is just an empty room with lots of shadows. There were about thirty people there, most of whom I recognized from David's ACT UP circles, including David himself, who was sitting alone in a chair with his arms folded tightly across his chest. People milled around uncomfortably for a few minutes until the service began, and then they just leaned against the bar and ordered beers because most of the women and the men had only been in that room before in association with beer and sex.

There's that strange pathology at memorial services where the person had to have been perfect. You're never allowed to mention any trouble or doubts you might have had about him. Robert was this tireless organizer and generally likable guy who had gone from being a Latin yuppie to a full-fledged radical. They showed television clips of him in a suit saying "Direct action works. It works." And later pictures of him, sick, standing on a fire escape on Gay Pride Day looking over the passing ACT UP contingent and waving a sign saying, "Audre Lorde is Love."

Then they showed all these slides of him doing this and doing that—usually at a demonstration or with his family in California or wearing some T-shirt with a slogan on it. But the unexpected sideline was that many of the slides also included handfuls of our other dead. Peeking over his shoulder or deep in conversation or carrying the other side of the banner was inevitably someone we'd already buried. Someone I'd met through David or at a benefit or rally and who I knew for a fact was dead. Plus all the others that I'd never met, but the silent shifting of feet registered their forgotten absence.

The end result was that when the slides were finished and it was time for people to come up to the microphone and say what they had to say about Robert, no one had anything to say. What I really mean is, no one wanted to talk. They just wanted to get the hell out of there. I saw Assotto Saint, skinny and drawn, saying to a friend, "Well, I'm still here." Then, when no one had anything to say, he stood up slowly and just left.

CHAPTER TWENTY-SEVEN

(IN WHICH DAVID REMEMBERS DON)

🍎 🍎 🍎 🍎

I WATCHED DAVID WALK UNSTEADILY DOWN FOUR-teenth Street and followed him for a bit, leaving Rita to go off to the bookstore. His head hung down below his shoulders like he just couldn't take it anymore. It was one of those most miserable walks of your life. I had no idea of what was the right thing to do and so ran after him, but slowly. He saw me and stopped to greet hello but was unable to wipe off the terror and misery. Absolutely incapable of hiding it.

We ended up at his house sitting on the bed and in the artificial light I could see how much damage the last few months had done. His skin was all dry and scaly, his face was ruddy from peeling. He had KS on one of his eyelids and he kept sweating profusely throughout the entire visit. Worse was how skinny he'd gotten. To that point where all their clothes are falling off but have to be loose to avoid swelling. It just hangs on their bodies kind of shapeless and you could tell he'd had hours and hours of diarrhea. Hours of crying on the toilet seat, alone in the middle of the night. Rectum raw and chafed, his guts sore from shitting without any sleep.

"Last month was my birthday," he said. "I turned thirty-five."

"Happy birthday," I said.

"I've been doing a lot of writing," David said. "About my earlier life. I've been jotting down little things worth remembering and trying to put them in some kind of order. Some of the most important things that ever happened to me. Some of the things that I want to have represent me when I'm gone."

"Do you want to read one to me?" I asked.

"This one is about my dead boyfriend Don," he said, going slowly through piles of disheveled papers, sweat cascading from his face, literally pouring all over himself and the paper. I watched it dripping and was utterly repulsed. I didn't want to be, but honestly, I was. I felt like I was going to throw up—the way you want to vomit at the smell of homeless people even while having nothing against them and a great deal of pity.

"One day Don and I went to the country and made love on the grass. I lay there, looking up at the sun and when I glanced over, Don was standing, nude and silent. I looked admiringly and saw a tree in Donny's ass. That is to say, I saw Don as a tree and then I looked at a real tree for comparison and saw it, suddenly, as a curvy, softy thing, like my beloved's joyful buttocks. Then I saw that thought in an objective way and saw the tree literally in Don's ass—protruding brightly from his rectum while he stood like a tree himself and then the sun got caught in my line of vision and it was over. One of those loving flashes of moment that become memories and that disappear from the collective unconscious when its rememberer dies too young because fate has frowned on all us young trees and God has taken our playmates away from us."

And all I kept thinking was that I wanted Troy to love me enough that I would never have to speak to my family again.

CHAPTER TWENTY-EIGHT

(IN WHICH KILLER INTRODUCES TROY RUBY
WHO THEN DESCRIBES HOW SHE
BECAME AN AMERICAN ARTIST)

🍎 🍎 🍎 🍎

"THE DYNAMICS OF GRAVITY," WAS ALL TROY SAID when I told her what had happened. Only I withheld the part about her and my family in case it didn't work out that way. I didn't want to have to be embarrassed. That was about six months ago when I still wasn't sure.

Troy was born in Cincinnati, Pennsylvania, in 1958 when Dwight David Eisenhower was president, and remains unresolved, just like the fifties. America jumped from World War II right into Vietnam and never made peace with those twenty years of betrayal. Our own Cultural Revolution. You look at the names of those who squealed on their friends — they became America's favorite heroes. The squealed upon rode off into nowhere and died in oblivion, never having been publicly redeemed. No punishment for the evil. No honor for the defiled. A model for the new age.

Her father, Joe-Jack Ruby, was night manager of the

Queen of the Nile Cafe in downtown Cincinnati, PA. Her mother was the resident songstress, Princessa De Barge. They picked her up at the age of two, grabbed all the cash in the till and came up to New York City on December 12, 1960—five weeks before the inauguration of President John Fitzgerald Kennedy.

The whole family watched his coronation from a tavern in Queens before settling into a small apartment in Greenwich Village sometime soon after.

Can't you see why I'm so taken by her?

Her story is so full of what was once considered romantic. And she told it to me the first time we fell in love.

"Robert Frost, crusty old codger," she said, leaning up naked against the dusty brick wall. "He stood, hatless in front of friendly television cameras that freezing afternoon and read his poetry, outside, to the nation. Then, in public schools from coast to coast, boys and girls, like you and me, Killer, we had to memorize his words. For Frost, though an artist, was a classy one. A classy American. Not some homo like Allen Ginsberg chanting *Sunflower Sutra* with little faggie pinkie cymbals."

At this point she assumed an imitative pose, stared off into the eye of an imaginary television camera and began recreating the gestures of Robert Frost fumbling with his scarf and notes at the 1960 presidential inauguration.

> *My little horse must think it queer,*
> *To stop without a farmhouse near . . .*

"Now, this couplet," she said. "Must have made a fierce impression, toddler that I was. Because years later, I would suddenly, as though channeling the spirit of the Creator, leap from my chair in a packed meeting hall and yell out, 'We're queer. We're near.' To which someone, I believe it was Maxine, responded, 'We're here, we're queer. Get used to it.' "

She lit a cigarette, held it posed up in the air, like a proper lady used to dirty work. Ashtray balancing precariously on the bed.

"See Killer, see how American culture is born. From Bob Frost to my lips. One long wagon train full of cottonmouth. Two hundred and eighteen years of collective unconsciousness. Next thing you can guess, some little fairy from Aimes, Iowa, will be jumping up and down rhyming *Seven years ago* and *homo* without any idea of how that free association was made. But the rhyme will sit comfortable, soothingly, in the psyche of its proprietors. Four score, I mean, for sure."

When comparing lovers there are subtle differences. One caresses me with more confidence but what does that really mean? Could it just be because her hands are bigger? Or is she really less fearful? Women have so many reasons to hesitate. One presses her lips to mine longer. She holds my thighs. Won't let me sleep. Lovemaking isn't my responsibility with one of them. It will come to me without worry.

"So, that was my role in the growth of Queer Nation," Troy Ruby told me, chomping on her cigarette. "One minor character in a minor moment. *Queer* did get old very fast, nowadays only academics take it seriously. But *Nation* managed to live on in many fond conversions. Transgender Nation, Alien Nation, Reincar Nation. And all along the line no one noticed how much that word echoed with the secret store of nostalgic desire for normalcy, normalcy, normalcy. Those apple pie, warm kitchens and American flags that are trapped somewhere back there between the hypothalamus and the frontal lobe. Someplace in the Central Drawer where *One* Nation *Under God, Indivisible, With Liberty and Justice For All* resonates eternally. And that is why *Nation* is ultimately such a comforting word. And that is how I became an American poet."

CHAPTER TWENTY-NINE

(IN WHICH TROY RUBY WRITES AND RECITES
A LOVE POEM FOR KILLER)

I T IS A VERY STRANGE THING BUT THE LESBIAN COMMU-
nity is a community of liars. Liars and believers, tops
and bottoms, butches and femmes, doers and wannabes, yup-
pies and deadbeats, mommies and daddies, enemies and
friends. It is all so dynamic.

The more you hide, the safer you are, especially if
you're out. When you're out, you're huge because this just
can't be. I'm so big, I'm enormous. How can I ever be happy
with little things? Sitting in someone else's backyard or on a
rooftop or fire escape, watching my lover, tanned, stretched
out on the chaise longue from Lamston's, gin and tonic, cigarette. Her arms are my greatest pleasure. Her legs are so
shapely. I love them.

"Killer," she said on the sixth night. "You know I have a
girlfriend, named Anita. You know that we have been together for seven years. I've told you that, right?"

"Yes," I said.

"She's a loving person. I admire her. She accepts me. She's fun. I like sharing things with her. She's easy to get along with."

"Sounds doomed," I said.

"Why?"

"She'll never be able to break down your isolation."

She leaned back in the bed and opened her legs a little.

"Troy?" I whimpered.

"Yeah?"

"Honey, could you hurt me? Rough me up a little?"

"What do you want?"

"I don't know, choke me, slap me, tell me off, make me cry. I really need to cry."

That night both of us were ashamed. Not only showing our masochism but even worse, not being able to really do it well. We made love again in the bathtub and her halfhearted thrashing became a faded memory.

"Hey," she said disengaging from my orgasm. "Let me get a cigarette, a cup of coffee and then I'll return to worship at the altar."

An hour later she recited a poem.

FOR KILLER
by Troy Ruby

Your head is a silk factory. Your forehead is a plum. Your eyes are ladles. Your mouth is a lamp. Your throat is a tortoise. Your theater is a snapping one. Your shoulders are a bowl of rum. Your chest is a radio. Your belly is mellow. Your pubic hair is tender. Your vagina is familiar. Your legs are red. Your feet are a mind.

Your ears are posies. Your nose is Kamchatka. Your cheeks are bonanzas. Your neck is a steam table. Your breasts are amusing. Your navel is paprika. Your timing is three-quarters. Your spaciness is ninety. Your ass is a cream stone. Your back lives in Manhattan. Your thighs can sing opera. Your knees are blue kanten. Your ankles are imported. Your toes are like string.

Your follicles are tremendous. Your scalp grows six feet. Your cerebrum came from Macy's. Your molars took a shine. Your gum bleeds like my salary. Your tongue stings of K-Y. Your chin sat on a platter. Your armpit is a springboard. Your waist told a secret. Your soft lips give me pleasure. Your clitoris winked in Technicolor. Your calves ate only vegetables.

"That's great," I said.
"You probably think it's a little long."

"Well," I said. "You could cut it down to just two stanzas."

"True."

"Troy?" I asked. "Do you think you can make it as a poet?"

"Never," she said. "I have other plans."

"Like what?"

"I've been doing research," Troy said. "I just started reading this new popular novel, *Good and Bad*, by Muriel Kay Starr."

"Not you too," I answered, bored. "Everywhere I go I see that fucking book."

"Well, excuse me."

"It's just that, we all know Muriel Starr," I tried to explain calmly. "She used to know Rita about ten years ago. Then she went out with this girl Lila Futuransky—who ended up involved in a scandal, but Muriel, of course, escaped unscathed. She moved to another neighborhood and got closer to power. Now she's got this novel out everyone is reading, but I hear it is really closeted."

"I read the first four chapters," Troy said. "And it made a lot of things very clear."

"About?"

"About the key to success."

"What are you going to do, Troy?" I asked.

"Well," she said, in her pinstriped and fedora tone of voice. "I'm writing a self-help book."

"I need self-help," I said.

"Well, then," she answered softly. "You'll be the first recipient."

CHAPTER THIRTY

(IN WHICH TROY RUBY ATTEMPTS TO WRITE A
BESTSELLER, AFTER READING FOUR CHAPTERS
OF *GOOD AND BAD*, BY MURIEL KAY STARR)

🍎 🍎 🍎 🍎

THE MILLENNIAL MOMENT:
Facing the Coming Millennia with Joy
by Troy Ruby

AMERICANS ARE SPIRITUALLY EXHAUSTED. WE HAVE
undergone a stressful millennia. Stresses of all kinds
have plagued the people of the earth. Too many to list here.

There have been famines, plagues, wars and strife of all
kinds. Unfettered strife, dominating the planet. In order to
avoid more strife of this nature, we must seize the Millennial Moment.

It is time for Americans to rest. The Millennial Moment is
one in which you can both seize and rest. Why have these two
activities been separated in the public imagination for so long?

Many of you face turning to your most productive
midlife years at the Millennial Moment. What does it mean?

Regular anxiety is bad enough, do we need to have Millennial Angst now too? The answer lies in the Eight Leaps of Faith. Just memorize them and you will have accomplished at least one thing. A mere glance at the Eight Leaps of Faith might even do a little something.

The Eight Leaps of Faith
The First Leap: The Past Is Prologue
Everything that is behind you should be equally behind.
The Second Leap: Reaching Your Goals
All previous goals must be dispensed with. Those who were first will now be last. The old order is rapidly changing. Set new goals. Only ones that you are sure you can reach without much luck.
The Third Leap: Every Generation Has to Try Heroin
Who are these people with whom we have lived on this planet for twenty-five years or less? Baby-Boomers. The key to the millennium lies in figuring out what they are going to be afraid of. The answer? The future.
The Fourth Leap: What About the Future?
We are all terrified that we are going to be punished.
The Fifth Leap: Finances
Buy stock in Prozac. Invest in the depression market and then get out. Then put all your money in the joy market. There are so many antidepressants competing for consumer dollars, but no one is selling depressants. Be an innovator. (See *Eighth Leap*.)
The Sixth Leap: The Decade of Exposure
Parity at the millennium. More exposure then for those with less now.

And vice versa.

The Seventh Leap: Pharmaceutical Publishing

There will be more books to promote pharmaceutical products.

The Eighth Leap: Is Prozac a Mood Alterer? AA Wants to Know

If AA is going to outlaw Prozac, AA won't be long for this world. (See *Sixth Leap*.)

Now for an important question.

Prince said he's gonna party like it's 1999. Do you think that you will be partying in 1999? Or will you be meditating?

To make your choice, order Troy Ruby's cassette tape and guide to how to meditate at a party. Just send $99.95 and keep your fingers crossed.

CHAPTER THIRTY-ONE

(IN WHICH TROY DESCRIBES NEW JERSEY AND
GOES TO GET A CUP OF COFFEE)

🍎 🍎 🍎 🍎

"TROY?" I ASKED, FULLY REINVIGORATED BY THE thought of the new age. "When did you first realize that you were in love with me?"

Troy sat back in the saddle, her cowgirl/aviator eyes. Her hips, lips, jaw slung slack like a fast train to Denver. All-American waffles and coffee in an old metal pot made on an open fire.

"It took me five hours of sitting on a Greyhound bus, bored and exhausted, before I could actually have a feeling. And then I realized what had really come true. I am so in love with you. I'm old enough now to know what love is. To recognize it."

"What happened on the bus?" I asked. "Where were you riding?"

"It was New Jersey, in January. Rolling industrial tundra where cancer is king. You know what I mean, Killer. Where every day of your life is 1962 and the dairy truck still rattles along a hardworking, run-down street. Kentucky Fried Chicken looks so old-fashioned in the graying dusk from a passing bus. Snow is resting on the eaves of small houses. Aluminum siding on a four-by-four square lot. Ho-hum. New Jersey.

"Some guy's got a machine shop over there. His boy is in the army. His girl does not want to get pregnant. The army's filled with fags now. Better off to keep your boy home. Go to Kentucky Fried Chicken feeling like an old-timer. It reminds you of your youth. A life in the history of advertising. Every logo had its moment. Even the countryside is dreary. Stomping ground for traveling oldies revivals. The Marvelettes are sixty. Still singing, *Mister Postman, please. Please bring me my social security check. I'm an aging Marvelette passing through New Jersey on a bus out of New York.* There's not one person who I envy in that entire state."

"And that's when you fell in love with me?"

She was so handsome, beautiful. My boy, my sailor. Tadzio meets Querelle. Dirty, sexy blue eyes. Soft lips sink ships. It was strange, what was happening. I just assumed it was a purely romantic image—a pretense of falling in love with a beautiful, smart, sexy, talented, interesting woman and her falling in love with me. And then, at some point, she decides that she wants to be with me forever. And then, just at that point, usually I would notice that she was able to cry and have temper tantrums and little moments of breakdown and vulnerability and I was not able to do so. Therefore, I had to leave her since I was not being conquered and remained emotionally brain dead.

All the while, though, I kept pretending I was really just some woman living in a ball of confusion pretending to be a lady-killer, but being very usual instead. Then, one day, as Troy was loving me, I realized that I was exceptional. That I was that strange ball of fire on whom romantic figures are traditionally based. I realized that I will never be alone for very long. I will never be bored and I will always be loved. I had to come to terms with the fact that I am sexy and I am easy to love. And it hit me, like a comet, that underneath all the huge waves of pleasure and all the passion and beauty and wonderful experiences and all the new ideas and emotions traveling with me, underneath all of that there might be this GASP pathology that has something to do with gay people and our families. How they have abandoned us and so we remain isolated. Yet, Troy can love me despite what America has done to us.

True, straight people do have all the other problems that we have. Especially being plagued by their own resentful selves as we are plagued by them. But they have not felt their own boots on their necks. Yet whenever I think about these facts, I worry about being glib and not noticing the impending sea of sadness that will be revealed as a moon crater ready to envelop my entire persona i.e., my world. When I notice that this crash has not happened yet, I worry that it will happen, should happen, must happen because it is hard to believe that a person can have had as much joy and pleasure and interesting moments as I have had and not await punishment.

"Honey," she said. "I'm going to the corner to get a cup of coffee."

CHAPTER THIRTY-TWO

(IN WHICH KILLER HAS A REVERIE ABOUT
POVERTY AND SHE AND TROY PLAY
WORD/LOVE GAMES)

🍎 🍎 🍎 🍎

"GET ME ONE TOO," I SAID, SIMULTANEOUSLY worrying about my finances, hoping that she would also buy a couple of doughnuts so I could have something to eat. In preparation for my visit with my beloved I had scraped together the cash for a deluxe chicken liver dinner. These ingredients were now waiting in the fridge. One dollar's worth of chicken livers. Rice. Thirty-five cents' worth of fresh mushrooms from the farmers market. One onion. She returned from the store with four coffees and a box of chocolate-covered doughnuts.

"What happened at the store?" I asked.

"Saw a rat," she said. "Then I was upset and wanted something special. So, I asked the storekeep if he had Diet Cherry Seven-Up or Wild Cherry Diet Pepsi. But he only had Crystal Cola Clear Pepsi. Not even Diet Crystal Cola Clear Pepsi. He did have Diet Dr Pepper, Diet Mandarin Orange

Slice, Caffeine-Free Sprite and Grape Gatorade. So, I got a box of doughnuts instead. I mean we could sit around eating hearts of palm and blood-red cherry tomatoes if you wish."

"What do hearts of palm taste like?" I asked.

"Like canned asparagus."

Between us there were few of the usual barriers. I had the chance to see her clearly. I guess it is this choice between being partial or being complete with other people you love. I guess mixture is the desirable state.

"Baby," I said, "choose your desirable state of choice from the following list."

"Okay."

"Mixture. Tundra. Beaucoup. Remo. Remoulade. Satay."

"My Way."

"At least you're honest," I said. "Your turn."

"Okay," Troy said, stretching her torso out over my world. "Okay, Killer, pick a phrase from the following list."

"I'm ready."

"Shark shards glistening. Lava raven so fine. Voodoo mixture Rambette."

"Ooh, baby be mine."

I ate three doughnuts in a state of deep shame. I don't have very much money for food right now. It is not that I don't eat. I do. I just don't have enough money for a free choice of food. I have to eat a lot of the same thing. I don't end up hungry at the end of the day but I do spend a lot of time imagining different tastes and treats. Like a piece of cake. A piece of cake filled with white cream.

"Last year I had a scare in the middle of April where I was living on a two-dollars-and-fifty-cents-a-day food budget. And I thought SHIT and got very depressed."

"Rice omelettes?" she asked tenderly.

"Yeah, and banana omelettes and rice and beans and bean omelettes, and beans and bananas and bananas and rice. And tea in coffee shops with lots of sugar and lots of milk."

"That is very hard to live with."

Something about her kindness and the coffee turned me on. I was overcome by sexual fantasies about her—all of which had nothing to do with her tenderness. She held me and caressed me and kissed me with real feeling but I wouldn't let go of the desire for something more. How strange to fantasize about your lover while she's actually there pleasing you. It got stranger and stranger. Her hands were all over me, caressing me through my shirt and I refused to respond, becoming more and more limp. Imagining, imagining, imagining. I wanted her to ask me what I wanted so I could ask for it at her bidding. But her silent caressing was deafening, silencing me, and I became angrier and angrier.

CHAPTER THIRTY-THREE

(IN WHICH THERE IS ANGER, SEX AND PREDICTIONS ABOUT AMERICA'S FUTURE)

♡ ♡ ♡ ♡

SHE'S NUDE. I'M CLOTHED. SHE WRAPPED HER CUNT around my leg and I could feel it leaving that dried white stain to be noticed later on the subway. She started fucking me but I wouldn't let her. She tried to make me come but I refused to do it.

"Tell me what you want to do to me and I'll let you," I said. "Tell me that you want to fuck me and I'll let you fuck me. Tell me that you want me to come and I will come."

"Do I have to say it?" Troy whined.

She paused and sighed a sigh of resolve. Amateurishly, but with great love and no desire, she grabbed my wrists and fought with me. I was so angry I could have punched her. I clenched my teeth. She bit my neck until I thought her teeth would break. Thank God. I like it when it hurts. Vaginal trauma is what I live for. Skeletal friction first and then my skin is the softest skin. When she comforted me, I loved the comfort. When she hurt me, I loved the pain. When she con-

126

trolled me I loved the capitulation. When she serviced me I loved the intent. Coming out is not the end of insanity, you know. It is only the beginning.

"You're not evil," she said.

"Call me Satan."

"I'll call you satin."

"I'm so excited about my future," I said.

"Future is a scary word here in America," she said, putting on her spurs. "Americans are dangerous, Killer. We destroy the earth, mind and lymph node and then market that destruction. We make it sound groovy. I have a lot of predictions about the future of America. Predictions that might have already come true."

"Like what?"

"I predict that there will be a new kind of cancer and advertising executives will name it Lymphomania. I predict T-shirts that say *I want to rape you*. I predict haphazard memorial services at every hour of the day and night because too many people are dead. Their ghosts have to compete wildly for remembrance. I predict that homeless people will piss on bank machines like storefronts lined with urinals."

"And personally?"

"First I lost my country. Now I predict that my country is going to lose me. Hmmmm. I'm suspicious."

"Of what?"

"You."

"Why?"

"Killer, you're too quiet to be trusted."

"What do you mean?"

"You're too selfish to talk."

"As Bob Dylan said, 'It's not my cup of meat.'"

"Well," Troy said. "I'm just Joe Lesbian on the street. I'm in love with you and I want to be with you. This is what Billie Holiday sings about. It's that dangerous netherworld called *really living*. Hey, I just thought of the first line of a new poem."

"What?"

"Roses are dead."

Troy's mouth is wired for sound. The nations of the world surrender to her beauty. She is penetration in public places. She is unisex to me.

CHAPTER THIRTY-FOUR

(IN WHICH VAN GOGH AND MUSKOGEE,
OKLAHOMA BOTH MAKE AN APPEARANCE)

🍎 🍎 🍎 🍎

"TELL ME," I SAID SWEETLY. "TELL ME, TROY, WHAT
kind of women do you usually like?"

"I used to have a stock answer," she said. "I like women
who are not too pretty, kind of insecure, good in bed and
butch enough to do me."

"That's about ninety percent of the lesbians in New
York City."

"Well," she said. "Then God bless New York City."

And all I could think about was how I had given up my
key to the world for the sake of my twat. On the other hand, I
actually think I am led around more by my mouth than I am
by my own genitalia. If I was a man I'd be a real cocksucker,
always at your service. Oh, wait a minute, women do that too.
It seems so unnatural.

"Another thing about America," she was saying. "I saw
these ladies getting off of the bus in Muskogee, Oklahoma.
They looked like East Village drag queens. Every fashion de-

cision they made that morning was predetermined by some nice gay man."

"Icky," I said. "The unconscious fag hags are everywhere. Now the insomnia begins."

"Insomnia?"

"Yeah," I said. "What else is worse than boredom? I'm so surprised that you fell in love with me, Troy. But it is so delicious. What a carcass on you, girlfriend. What a massive slab of beef."

"There was a really beautiful Puerto Rican woman in the store this morning," Troy said. "She also saw the rat."

"How come Spanish women look divine in something that would make any white girl look like trash?"

"Because, Killer, you have a double standard. You see something tacky on a Spanish girl and you think it belongs there. Admit it, and then get over it."

Where I live is just an apartment but it is airy. Icy, with illusory sky and high-ceilinged blue. I like living in a blue room because Van Gogh had beautiful blue rooms in that painting. Van Gogh's room.

Troy was making my deepest wish come true. She was watching me and seeing me and telling me hard to face, difficult unpleasantries about myself that I would never otherwise know. That is really what I want from another person.

One of the things that I love is a hot summer night. A hot winter night. The sound is blowing in your hair instead of breeze. There are two candles—purity and passion, and purity burns out while passion is just getting started. It's exciting.

"I'm excited," I said. "I think I had too much coffee."

"Here baby," she said. "Smoke a cigarette. It helps drain some of the oxygen away."

I feel the way I feel when I'm sitting home alone in the dark and I can't even listen to the radio because everything is too sensitive. It is so romantic.

Will I stay in bed reading in the morning while my lover sleeps beside me? The trees outside my window. My tattoo. Her book. Will I bustle, bring her coffee? Read the paper silently? Comment on an article and happen to look up? Her body there before me. Sitting sipping coffee. Eating bread so slowly. Hair unkempt. Feet bare.

If you sit before the ocean or on a balcony in Chelsea and the city lives before you and the sea and still beyond. There are moments of discomfort when the cold wind blows too sharply or I don't know how to hold her or I can't show my joy. But in between those moments there is a luscious disappearance. She folds into my armchair. I forget I'm on the sand.

CHAPTER THIRTY-FIVE

(KILLER'S SOLILOQUY)

🍎 🍎 🍎 🍎

ALONE HAS SUCH A DIFFERENT FEELING NOW. IT IS all about waiting for you. There's jazz on the radio, I have a quiet glass of water. The clock says eleven o'clock and I'm waiting for the phone to ring announcing that you've been to work, been home and are now ready for me. It is a different kind of anxiety, this emptiness. Surrounded by my papers, my mementos, tchotchkes, all artifacts from my life before you. I wait, never patiently as you take your time. I have more of it—more time for rumination. Every day this girl is filled with feeling—wanting to tell you all, and still hesitating. Not wanting to say the wrong thing, never to lead myself into a path of commitments, all of which rest, currently, on the tip of my tongue. These cigarettes are deadly, just smoke them to pass the time. Where are you, Troy? Your touch works on my flesh like a respirator, like Vick's Vaporub. Like a samba when you're feeling free enough, or the sun without boredom or one final glass of beer. I speak my love for you over and over again, but that vocabulary is so limited by words I've heard before—so it's a tense repetition. Speaking love the same way to the same girl night after day.

The radiator whistles. There are holes in the walls of these old tenements. When it really chills outside I can't get warm. Night creeps from all corners. You're the kind of woman that girls want to own. It's so obvious, the possession. You've got a permanent black collar around your neck. Keeping way too busy is the only form of escape that you know. Can I please be your wife? Even if only for a few days. Then I'm sure to be filled with regret and try to set you free unwillingly. Thirty years old and now restraint is so hard to muster. Hey, girlfriend, where are you? My jaw is locked in anticipation. Phone? Ring? Ring! Why don't you? Your arrival is obvious. Why can't I just relax and wait for it? Ho-hum. Yours is the last phone call every night. And it is a guarantee.

Okay, you called. You're on your way. At least a half hour from a store on Thirty-ninth Street unless you take a cab. What else to do but clean out my supplemental dictionary or else try to figure out how to alphabetize on my 1980 IBM computer. How can I figure out anything if I don't know what "field" means. Oh, you're here. Hooray.

I can smell you when you're only halfway up the stairs but even that warning doesn't anticipate the delight at your appearance. We embrace, sit together, chat softly. I bring you something, something to drink. I have been holding on to an emotion, trying to figure out how to offer it—to offer you a tip of an iceberg as bait to my life. Finally it comes out carefully, seems to appear haltingly. I wait for some recognition but there's an associative silence instead. Whatever it was I said only reminded you of your own sadness. It brought up something hidden which is now occupying your mind.

CHAPTER THIRTY-SIX

(IN WHICH KILLER RECEIVES A LETTER)

🍎 🍎 🍎 🍎

"WHAT IS IT, BABY?" I ASK SOFTLY. "COME ON, JUST tell me." Because I want so desperately to be close to you. I'm trying every way I can.

"Oh," she said. "I was coming over here and I saw a woman who looks exactly like Anita. You know, that dark, wild kind of beauty. It made me feel so guilty and upset, missing her. When you've been with someone that long, losing them is indescribable. It is like cutting off half my body. It is like I lost myself and I don't know what's left."

"Oh," I said.

"I feel so awful," Troy said, "for all the bad ways I've treated her. For all the mistakes I've made. For all the ways I've hurt her and haven't treated her right. I come home at night and listen to the answering machine. Every night, waiting to see if there will be a message from her. I mean I can't be the one to call her, it would be like torturing her. I can't be the one but my life is incomplete without her. My greatest fantasy is that she would be in my life every day and I have to find a way to have that because having that would be having everything and without that I . . . I don't know."

"Oh."

God, my apartment looks so shabby. I'm ashamed of it. My clothes are all hand-me-downs. I'm deeply ashamed. Where is my father? I haven't heard from him since April. He and my mother came over to the house. We were sitting around watching the TV news. My mother brought over some Cypriot food. I guess it was around the Greek Easter. *Domaldos*. Little cakes. Rita came by, stayed for a second. Later my father called me up admonishing me for hanging out with dykes. I guess he forgot that talk we once had. It is so hard to defend myself to my own father when there is nothing to defend. But, like every child I desperately want him to love me, so I sit, stupidly, trying to explain. There is no explanation. Only, now, after the subsequent nine months of silence, can I see that he didn't call for an explanation. He called for an excuse.

Sometimes it seems too obvious that women are replaceable. I don't like feeling that way but I often do. You love one then you love another. Each one is different and eventually you stick with one or you don't. They have the same pros and the same cons. The ones that like me are naive, gullible, respond to praise, love permission, can never fully reciprocate because they are so goddamn insecure. That's the trap. The same reason they're grateful is why they can never give back. That's why Troy is my dream girl.

Three months into the silent treatment I wrote my mother a letter. I feared being shunned forever. I can sit here in my slum apartment in Manhattan, look for work, water plants, fall in love and they'll never know the difference. I wrote my mother a letter and asked her to love me. Here is what she said:

Dear Stella (My real name),

My background was more limited than yours. My opportunities were more limited and my experiences were more limited. My father and mother came here on a boat from Cyprus. I still do not fully understand American ways even though I have lived here my whole life.

As my first child, I was over-involved with you, hung on every achievement with incredible wonder and suffered with every distress as though it was my own. It was too much and I knew that I needed to dilute our relationship. To normalize it. But I guess I never did it good enough.

Now you are asking me to go against your father's will. I think you need to understand what your father has done for us. When my father died, he left my mother penniless. You may remember that in her will she left each grandchild thirty-five dollars. I think you used it to buy a pair of sneakers. There aren't too many people who would have taken in a mother-in-law to a three-room apartment while facing a new baby and a demanding job.

Daddy went beyond the line of duty in the way he took care of my mother, me and my children. I will always be thankful for that.

Your father and I are old now. He is sixty-eight years old and I am sixty-five. We are not going to live forever. We want to enjoy our last years of our lives with as little tension as possible. You are so uncompromising. You are the one creating the problems.

> *Love,*
> *Mom*

"Anita was my life," Troy was saying. "You know, she's my family."

CHAPTER THIRTY-SEVEN

(IN WHICH A NEWLY EMPLOYED TROY TAKES KILLER OUT FOR COFFEE)

🍎 🍎 🍎 🍎

THERE I AM, 11:20 IN THE EVENING WAITING FOR MY beloved to appear at the door, on the evening of the fourth day of her new job, caked in white pastry flour and smelling of vanilla like Aunt Bea or some other pudgy nonentity. I am waiting for my female boyfriend. It's a beautiful night.

After work and a shower, Troy took me out for a cup of coffee at some strange place with burnt-orange shag carpets and two balconies. I was undergoing a temperament change — being curt, rude, lonely, saying *NO* to others. Everything going every which way.

The air was soothing, like flesh. The two combined put me in a coffee shop diva dream state. A painting of Santa Lucia holding her own eyes on a plate. Cafe con leche the real way. A little cup of espresso in a big glass of hot milk. I forgot to mention the Puerto Rican folk guitarist singing "Sloop John B" for some friends in the back.

Then we climbed the stairs for two suddenly expensive margaritas on the mouse-infested rooftop bar—walls painted luscious tangerine flesh. Spending money. Me realizing I'd better start budgeting and then me and Troy talking, her telling me something very special. Something I'd only imagined privately and thought I'd have to wait for. Eternally elongated secret hoping.

Now here is what she said, but I'll put it in parentheses which is the written version of a whisper.

(She said, "You shouldn't worry about Anita, Killer, because my relationship with you is already better than that one ever was—even though you and I have only known each other a very short time.")

"I'm in love with you and you'd better get used to it," she said.

After going home and making love we got into a critical discourse on Americana as global kitsch. We started going one for one with good American worldly contributions and bad. Every time she'd come up with some fantastic Americanist creation like Ornette Coleman, I'd come back with something equally banal like Epilady or Domino's Pizza. We finally converged on the question of Steve Lawrence and Edie Gormet and whether they were absurdly awful or absolutely fabulous depending on whether we were going by my egghead, beatnik, natural wood floor aesthetic or her green shag, East Village fag aesthetic—which we agreed was high on the list of America's greatest creations.

"I knew Clinton was going to be a dog from the televised inauguration parties," she said. "Especially when he had Aretha Franklin sing the theme song from *Aladdin*. It was all downhill from there."

"Well, who would you want to have perform at your inauguration?" I asked Troy wistfully.

"You know, something presidential. Like the Village People and Lorna Luft."

Then we went shopping on Avenue C buying Catholic/Chango tchotchkes and mangos. Bodega candles are part of generic Loisaida culture.

"God, I wish you could see the market in Mexico City," Troy said.

I've never been everywhere. I grew up in South Brooklyn between Avenues L and M. Lennon and McCartney.

"It's so beautiful," she said. "There are anal-retentive stacks of thousands of purple cloves of garlic in four or five varieties. Huge bales of sun-blanched corn husks and clear smooth banana leaves rolled out in even piles. Caught some guy with his hand in my back pocket. Piles of wet, brown móle like little towers of fresh shit. Dried fish the size of dragonflies. Wet green cactuses deneedled and raw. Watermelons with red gaping holes of invitation. Deep-fried eggs, fake carnations. Dried tamarinds. Tomatillos in light green husks. Tomatoes in rows like red, plastic teeth. Granadas. Mamey."

"What else?" I asked.

"El Aquario Fantastico del Mundo del Mar—which turned out to be a collection of fish tanks on the thirty-eighth floor of the Latino-Americano Building."

"Troy," I said. "I feel so close to you and I know you feel close to me."

All night we rolled around with animals underneath our lips. Troy had a snake wrapped around her teeth and I had a big rat, in honor of Rita, caught passively between my molars.

That day purple petals fell from the trees every time a light breeze blew.

"Ate tortillas soaked in red chilis with sour cream," she said. "White cheese."

CHAPTER THIRTY-EIGHT

(IN WHICH KILLER SEES THE BEAUTIFUL PEOPLE)

🍎 🍎 🍎 🍎

A FEW THINGS HAVE GONE ON SINCE THEN. OCCASION-ally Troy realizes one or more of her life's goals and I am peacefully happy each time. Purely happy where your facial muscles relax and the mirror loses your years. She is kind to me and loving to me but still looking back. I try to quell my jealousy. She keeps working at the wedding cake factory. I water plants. The rhythm of work. How hard it is to make a living. I'm not some middle-management wannabe. That's not the life for me. One great thing about work, after-wards I'm too tired to be anxious. I knew two girls named Ex-pression and Order. They were a perfect match. They met, fell in love and helped each other for the rest of their lives. Their home together was comfortable and warm.

One night we went to a party and both knew for unspo-ken certain that Anita would be there. I watched Troy put on the vest Anita gave her. I saw how much she still wanted to please her. She wore her gift on her chest like a blazing welcome sign. I became very quiet. Wait. When the day comes that too will pass. I will be filled either with rage or with joy. But until that moment I can't imagine which. *Leidenschaff, die Leiden Schafft.* That suffering which passion creates.

"Troy?" I said in bed last night. "How do you think you're going to die?"

"Oh, I don't know," she said. "Probably like Sam Cooke. You know, running naked through a hotel lobby chasing a white woman. Hey you, what do you want?"

"I want you to bind me," I said. "Gag me, blindfold me, beat me, fuck me and then I want you to kiss me."

The next morning I walked to Rita's house so that we could go over to the hospital together. My eyes were wide open — the whole city was a poem. There were young beautiful people everywhere drinking coffee. They're not THE BEAU-TIFUL PEOPLE. They're lovely.

CHAPTER THIRTY-NINE

(RED RIVER)

🍎 🍎 🍎 🍎

THE NEXT EVENING TROY AND I WERE SITTING AROUND watching TV.

"They hired a new manager today and it was not George," she said.

"Why not?"

"Because of his drinking. I told you. So, guess who got it?"

"Who?" I asked.

"Guess."

"Who?"

"GUESS!"

"You."

"No," she said. "Louise from purchasing. She wants to cut lunch from one hour to forty-five minutes. I told her, that's why it's called a lunch hour and not a lunch forty-five minutes."

The movie on TV was *Red River*.

"Look at that man ride a horse," I said.

"Tell me about your day," she said.

"It was boring. Tell me about yours."

"Well . . ."

"Sounds pretty boring."

I thought about a bowl of popcorn.

"Carole at the shop is pregnant," Troy said. "Don't tell anybody."

"Who am I going to tell?"

"Louise at work filed her nails. I painted my toenails Amethyst Smoke."

"You did?" I looked down at Troy's feet and ripped off her socks. "Oh my God, you painted your toes."

"Amethyst Smoke. Now he's gonna get it."

We looked back at the screen.

Then the intercom buzzed and Rita walked in.

"Hi lovebirds," she said, looking real strange. "I bought a six-pack. It's ten o'clock, time to come out and play. You guys are too much. Mind if I turn down the sound? I knew two girls like you once. They were real cute. One started seeing a boy and the other flipped out and left town. I drove her to the airport."

"Are you all right?" I asked.

"Sure," she said. "What are you two watching here?"

"John Wayne in *Red River*," Troy answered.

"That movie is so gay."

"No, it's not," Troy said.

"Yes it is," Rita answered, popping open a beer.

"Where?"

"When Montgomery Clift looks Big John longingly in the eyes and says 'I want to hold your gun.' Hey, let's put on a record. When did you stop buying records, Killer? 1963? Frank Sinatra? Goes great with John Wayne. Two famous assholes."

"No one's making you stay here," I said.

"Dave died," she said.

"Oh," Troy and I both said. And then we were all overcome by that moment for which there is no appropriate response except familiarity. It is shameful, not knowing how to really feel it. Being overprepared for death.

"I'll make some popcorn," Troy said and went into the kitchen.

"I wish I had a girlfriend," Rita said.

"Hey," Troy called in. "There isn't any popcorn."

"Look," Rita said, turning the channel. "Now this is a really great movie. This is a Frank Capra film. This is really funny."

PART FOUR

RATS, LICE AND HISTORY

CHAPTER FORTY

MRS. SANTIAGO AND I SAT, ANXIOUSLY STARING AT the old clock on the wall. Two minutes to nine. It was so quiet in the office you could hear bottles smashing on the sidewalk seventeen floors below.

At nine o'clock, on the nose, the Rat Commissioner would be releasing his new report to the city press corps and everyone at Pest Control and Food and Hunger had placed bets on which papers would run the story on the front page. Daily Double if you could pick the headline.

" 'A Good Year for Rats,' " predicted Mrs. Santiago. "Five dollars on *Newsday.*"

We all knew the report's contents by heart. The Health Department had found an 18 percent rise in rat sightings. They were trying to put it off on increased public awareness about vermin. But the facts were that the number of reported rat bites had also gone up and someone was going to have to pay.

From my point of view, the problem has to do, primarily, with the narrow scope of perspective that New Yorkers apply to rats, and occasionally to mice. They think it only happens here. New Yorkers are so myopic. They don't realize that at the exact second that they are watching rodents frolicking on the subway tracks, somewhere off in a faraway ocean, a weather-beaten fishing trawler is about to dock on a tiny island. Stowed away in the locker of that boat is a pair of one-pound Norway rats ready to scoot along the hawser when the sun goes down. At the same moment, deep in the hold of a neighborly grain barge, a family of Polynesian rats are about to come ashore. Once they've invaded the previously pristine spot, these rats are going to go after large unsuspecting birds by biting the backs of their necks, severing their spines and chewing off their legs. New Yorkers think this only happens to them.

Rats are an essential part of the history of the world. They are more influential than people. The dynamic between vermin and civilians, creators and destroyers, is the relationship most at the center of life. Everything else spins around it, because of it. There are Norway rats, genus *Rattus norvegicus*, which have lived and bred underneath New York City probably as long as humans have done so aboveground. Heaven and hell are just the metaphors.

Take me and Killer, for example. We are most comfortable living in neighborhoods where there are so many people walking around who would be locked up in institutions if they lived anywhere else. In relation to them, we feel normal. Same is true for the Norways. They are very partial to the moist underground conditions of lower Manhattan with its high water table and channeled rock and all those substructures dating back to the earliest days in the life of the city. We're all living together in our favorite part of town.

In my world a lot of people die young. They get AIDS or drugs or live dangerously. But some of the most decrepit street people seem to live forever. The most annoying ones live on and on. Like the filthy, emaciated white girl who wears a winter coat in the summer and shuffles along barefoot whining, "No one will help me because I'm white."

This approach doesn't really make you want to help her.

Or the really insane skinny black guy, also filthy, who wears a pair of pants over his head and always has mucus on his shirt. He sits in the middle of the sidewalk and says, "Excuse me, do you have any Grey Poupon?"

You just can't believe they're still living but year after year they are.

Sometimes I'll be walking down the street and I'll see a young gay man just moving along, minding his own business. Something in this guy's shirt or stance or facial expression will remind me of another gay man I used to know but haven't seen or heard from or thought about for months or years at a time. Suddenly, I will consider and then assume that he is dead and I will never see him again. Sometimes it will be a gay man whose name I barely knew and so it would be impossible to ask anyone after his whereabouts. At this point, I usually wonder why I am still alive and I worry about how much David must have hated me for outliving him. The envy of the dying for the living. I feel like one of those Super Rats.

There is no way to kill them. They are immune to everything except being hit over the head or shot. Once it became evident that no poison was ever going to get them, the guys at the lab came up with the most diabolical tactic ever attempted in the history of Rat vs. Human warfare. Warfarin. It is this odorless, tasteless, anticoagulant that produces massive internal hemorrhaging. Basically everything inside their bodies that holds and channels blood falls apart and the rats turn into one big, red, sloppy mess. Their bodies no longer have systems and just become containers for sloshy, directionless blood.

At first I wondered about the mind of the man who invented Warfarin. It seemed so treacherous. I wondered how he got the idea. But then it turned out that even this was not evil enough because the Super Rats were immune to that too. The Bureau instructed us to try zinc phosphide, next. A quick-acting poison that smells like garlic. But the rats detected it in the bodies of their dead friends and figured out pretty quickly how to stay away. Finally, they sent us out into the field with packages of Lorexa. This odorless overdose of vitamin D was exactly the recipe that sent the Super Rats to the gas chamber. The jig was up. But then the budget cuts came along.

The cold clock laboriously reached nine.

"New York Post," I called out. "Five bucks."

Mrs. Santiago glared over her eyeglasses. "I'll stay with *Newsday.*"

When the phone rang, we all jumped. But, when I picked it up it was Manuel on the other end, worked up into a frenzy over the food for the memorial service.

"Grapes will be fine," I said. "Something pure."

At Pest Control we can take off time for funerals, but when they come at the rate of one or two a week, Mrs. Santiago starts noticing disapprovingly. Her nephew got murdered in Bushwick last February and her brother got shot in the head in Puerto Rico in March. So, she tends to accept regular death in the lives of her employees. Her other sister's boyfriend died of AIDS in April but she didn't say much about that. I just think that sick days should be for when *I* am sick. I need separate leave days for everyone else. Plus one day a month for menstrual cramps.

"How are you doing?" I asked Manuel quickly.

"I am very very angry at those PWLOPWA's."

"What's that?"

"People Who Live Off People With AIDS. If this epidemic ever ends, everyone who is still alive will be suddenly unemployed."

"More histrionics?" I asked.

"I think they should change the name of this disease," he said. "From AIDS to AIDA. Only Leontyne Price can do it justice."

Even before David actually died, there was a fight over the body. Some people in ACT UP wanted to have a political funeral but Manuel didn't think that was dignified. He wanted something quiet. But there were more ACT UPers in David's care group than there were people like Manuel. So, they ended up with a weird and uncomfortable compromise of a public funeral, but a demure one. Manuel was so racked with guilt that he became obsessed with the funeral catering and called me three times the day before with a wide range of bizarre suggestions like portable hummus and Portabello mushrooms. I think he just wanted attention.

At times like this you have to sit down and ask yourself all kinds of questions:

What would David have wanted?

and

Is this for the living or for the dead?

Let's face it, David was a Liza Minnelli fag. This was the guy who used to find out where famous people went to Alcoholics Anonymous meetings so he could hold their hands during the serenity prayer. He would have wanted something fabulous.

David was cheated out of his life. That's one of the few items he had in common with his peers. He would have wanted something angry and hyperbolic. A fire or explosion. Something destructive. He would have really liked that.

David was a postmodern aesthete. He would have wanted something formally inventive but timeless.

Natural beauty? Kitsch classic? How do you choose?

CHAPTER FORTY-ONE

THE OFFICIAL STEPPING-OFF SPOT FOR THE FUNERAL was at Houston Street and First Avenue at five o'clock. But, the organizers forgot that about twenty-five homeless people sold their stuff on that very spot every day. There is no more public space in urban life. The people with no private space live in it. Then the city tells them that that is their private problem. So we all had to kind of stand around them, step over them and refuse them nonchalantly while crying and comforting each other at the same time.

No one knew what to say really because, apparently, there had been three other people from ACT UP who had died in the previous two weeks. So, the habitual mourners were sick of making cooing comforting sounds to each other. The endearments stuck in their throats. Besides, there is that special brand of communication that gay people utilize at AIDS funerals. The standing-around-in-sorrow-state-of-silent-acknowledgment method. We raise our eyebrows and nod. David told me once it was perfected in sex clubs. Like when he used to run into that uptown editor at some dive on the Upper West Side. The guy would be yelling, "Suck that dick. Suck that big dick." And when he would catch David's eye, up went those acknowledging eyebrows.

David's closest friends had accepted his death long ago. In fact, most had buried him emotionally while he was still registering a pulse. Those who came by word of mouth had their own reasons. They knew him or his writing vaguely. They had their own multitudes of dead that still needed to be mourned and so haunted other people's funerals as excuses to further grieve. Some were total fans of his writing and felt themselves to be in an underground historical moment that would surely have some latter-day significance when his reputation was exhumed from the mass grave into which it was now tossed. It was a cortege of reasons.

Lyle looked absolutely terrible. He earnestly handed out these horribly tacky bodega candles. Instead of pictures of Chango, the glass containers had pictures of David like he was some saint. I guess Lyle wishes *he* was a saint and really wants bodega candles with his own face on them when it is time for his funeral. I'll have to remember that. His boyfriend has been dead for two months and funerals like David's were just more practice until the day it was Lyle's turn to fall down in the next round of musical casket.

I stopped to talk to this black guy, Kurt, that David and I had run into at a party in Dyke Slope last year.

"What can you say?" I said.

"I'm so tired of this," he said.

Then we each moved on and said the same thing to someone else.

A couple of hundred people showed up which seemed like a lot, but actually it was very little. Especially when you consider the scope of David's reputation. There should have been more, at least. I know that he wanted his funeral to be the catalyst for the revolution. Who doesn't? And with each

AIDS funeral that possibility always lingers. But you can tell within the first ten minutes that it is not going to go that way. People were not furious. Just exhausted.

Finally, Ira drove up with a van and Manuel and some others lifted out the coffin. It was white, like cake frosting, with light blue trim. That really surprised me because I knew that David was Jewish, so I had expected a plain pine coffin like the one my mother had. But then I realized that Manuel had done the shopping and that tradition is something he just couldn't be expected to know. For the first time, I felt guilty. Maybe I should have done the shopping. Isn't that my responsibility, as a Jew?

A bunch of big, strong gym queens in tiny cutoffs lifted the coffin onto their shoulders and all two hundred of us walked behind it up First Avenue. There were some Radical Faeries with bells on their toes, but most people just held those awful candles. Some had photos of Dave that the Graphics Committee had made up and Killer had her own little personal photograph. Some people were carrying his books. Then I thought for the first time that his sales would probably go up dramatically for one day, now that the *Times* obituary had come out. Too bad they never reviewed him while he was alive.

There were not many observers on that strip of First Avenue as we walked past some funeral homes and into Tompkins Square Park. We ended up in the void where the bandshell used to be and everyone stood around while the event's organizers laid out a metal frame. They placed David's casket on it, right under a tree. Then they opened up the casket.

First he looked very familiar and it felt good to see him. I wondered if death was just getting too easy for me, or if seeing him dead was actually the peaceful thing. But then there was this wafting of embalming fluid and it was horrible. It didn't smell like dead, rotting animals. It smelled like chemistry, or the inside of the Xerox store. It smelled like something really awful for your lungs that just made everyone want to run away. But we all stayed and got infected by it and kept staring at him, lying there.

CHAPTER FORTY-TWO

IT DIDN'T TAKE LONG FOR THE JUNKIES AND HOME-less who hang out in the park to come over and check out what was going on. There were young guys and girls with beers in paper bags looking at his body. You could see them wondering about themselves since a lot of them have HIV too or other things like poverty and confusion, which also guarantee short life.

A bunch of Latin kids on bikes started riding around the body and they acted like they'd stared death in the face before because there was no awe in their curiosity. I noticed that the embalmer had covered up David's KS with makeup and somehow this was the most upsetting part of the whole scenario. It brought him back to the state before he was splattered by it, which reminded me, suddenly, of how he looked before he was really dying. The makeup made it all so palatable, peaceful. Cinematic.

Manuel stood up and read a poem that was pretty rambling and, frankly, a little boring. Later he sent me a copy without a note.

DAVID

David's body is a sweet, emaciated profile
against the twenty-first century. If a tree
is that century, his shadow barely cools the bark.
If his memory is a cake, it lies, dusty in
a bakery window on Fourteenth Street.
Young girls, ex-virgins, imagine its dried, crusty frame
through new eyes, imagine new life.

We who remain shuffle slowly to the subway.
We make time for death between life and rest.
We make time for three vignettes, or two well
cared for photographs, one reduced phrase,
one gesture and one sound. One memento, one tomato
one joke retold too often. One association, one pathetic
moment, one exciting sentence, one melody, one moon.
We suddenly recall, we forget, suddenly.

Manuel was crying so uncontrollably that between his sobs and his accent, I couldn't hear most of the piece anyway. I just watched him, like a spectacle. Next on the program were three people reading selections from David's books—all of which were somber. I always thought that his books were funny. But I guess you can't do that at a funeral. Following that, a guy from ACT UP made a political speech. Then a couple of friends said good-bye in different ways.

I was thinking over what I wanted to say. I had been trying to come up with something since before Dave was even dead. But nothing ever popped into my mind. It wasn't until I was standing there, with toxic lungs, that I realized that I had nothing to say. I realized that I was very, very angry at David when he died. Our relationship was so one-sided. He never thought about me until I was right in front of his face. Is that awful? To want mutuality from a dead man? I did not want to get up there in front of all that authentic, if convoluted, feeling and pretend things had been different than they were. I too have grief.

So, I passed.

Killer did get up though and said some sentimental things that actually moved me. So, I had my catharsis. By proxy.

"I remember a story David once told me about his childhood," she said. "He was always telling stories, especially toward the end of his life. And I guess that, as a writer, that was the best way for him to convey his feelings. Anyway, once when he was about eight and his sister was about ten, they went to their aunt's house on Long Island and spent the night in a tent in her backyard. Being city kids, there was some anxiety and concern about sleeping 'outside' and David was particularly concerned about spiders.

"After they pitched the tent, he decided that the best way to protect himself and his sister from these spiders would be to build some kind of obstruction. So, he went back in the house and got a broom and swept a foot and a half area all around it. Then they collected stones and bricks and pieces of wood and built a little fence around the swept area. But, still not convinced that this was protection enough, David and his sister jumped up and down, up and down singing, 'Out spiders out. Out. Out. Out.' And then he finally felt safe enough to go to sleep.

"I keep thinking," she said. "About how he equated health with going to sex clubs. So that even when he had real problems with his legs, he would go and let everyone know that he had gone. Make a big deal out of it. I guess that ever since he was a little boy, David needed rituals. He needed magical thinking and mutual experiences. He very much wanted to live and he needed to feel that he had done everything he could to take care of a situation, even if it was unmanageable."

The sunlight whispered through the petals of rickety old survivor trees. The park looked really beautiful.

The next act was a flute, followed by the requisite recording of Nina Simone played off of someone's boom box. By this time in the proceedings, people started to look at their watches because they had places to be and death is not enough of an anomaly.

Then someone announced that David's father was there. This made his few real friends turn around in surprise because everyone knew how much his father had hurt him. He turned out to be this graying Jewish lawyer, in his mid-sixties. Kind of upper-middle-class. He was wearing a summer suit and a tie and really he was the only person in the park wearing formal dress. He was totally out of place. I was kind of surprised that the old man would show up at something like this. Show his face at this late date. But that thought was quickly replaced with the realization that he had no understanding of what we knew or felt about him. He did not believe that we existed. He did not know his son had relationships.

Dave's dad walked up to the front of the crowd and stood between us and the coffin. He didn't look at Dave while we were all watching, but he did stand next to his son's body. Quiet shapes, under the tree. Then he took this folded piece of paper out of his breast pocket and adjusted his glasses.

"My son, David Gabriel Berman, was born on February twenty-second, 1958. George Washington's birthday. We promised him that all his life, his birthday would be celebrated as a national holiday. But then they changed the law and George Washington's birthday was no longer celebrated on February twenty-second. David accepted this without complaint, just as he later accepted having AIDS without complaint. David graduated magna cum laude, Phi Beta Kappa from Columbia University and lived for a year in Portugal and for a year in Rome, Italy. I am sorry and will always be sorry that David is no longer with us. So long, Dave."

There are rarely any parents whenever we all meet. And their sudden appearance immediately deprives us of our collective adulthood. We know they are against us and it is so hard to maintain stature in the presence of your fiercest opposition. Even when we are so beautiful and strong.

In the silence that followed, nobody even gasped. Some people looked at each other and raised those eyebrows, but most of us were not surprised. We're so used to it. We're so used to parents who show up at the last minute and never took the time to know their child. Who have no idea of who they are talking about. We suffer them silently.

We took Dave's father personally because most of us know our families would do the same. The most common link between all gay people is that at some time in our lives, often extended, our families have treated us shabbily because of our homosexuality. They punish us, but we did not do anything wrong. We tell each other about this all the time but we never tell the big world. It is the one secret not for public consumption.

We'll stand up proudly on television in slave collars and penis tucks but we will never speak out publicly about what our families have done to us. It is too true.

After Dad, a gay guy, a real queen, who had gone to Columbia with Dave read the Kaddish and all the Jews started to cry. What a switch from Dad to hear this quiet, gay Jew in hot pants and a tallis, whine our friend's dark death in a five-thousand-year-old tongue. We are old. We do exist. We can mourn. We do have language. We still have that. Finally, I was able to be afraid.

CHAPTER FORTY-THREE

POST-FUNERAL IS ONE OF THOSE STILL UNDEFINED moments. Sometimes you rush off to another appointment and the whole thing only hits you that night, in bed, or during a vaguely familiar feeling at the next funeral. Sometimes, though, we all go off for drinks.

The day of Dave's funeral was, weatherwise, a great one, so I decided to take a stroll downtown looking for a comfortable spot in the beachfront cottage called my erotic imagination. And, after all, that night did become a balmy night. Everywhere I turned, people were chattering with pleasure through open windows and there was a clatter of forks against plates. Beer bottles against glasses.

I walked over to this specialty cinema on the other side of town because I had vaguely heard that there were some gay movies from Cuba playing there. I thought that maybe a certain Cuban might be waiting in front.

Having an hour to kill, I took a seat in the rear garden of an old-fashioned West Village restaurant and sat alone at a round, green table, ordering a green alcoholic drink. The place was totally empty and I was feeling strangely elated, perforated. So, feeling very private, I decided, on a whim, to forego the margarita and order a Coors beer instead. Now, the Coors boycott has been on for so long, due to their support of right-wing causes, that I had never in my life actually tasted one. I was looking forward to the experience, but still felt a little strange when the bartender served it up in the can. I felt a little ashamed, sitting there drinking a can of Coors.

As the drink progressed the novelty wore off and I began to feel weird. I got up from my chair and chased down the bartender, who was reading a newspaper in the cool inside, to ask him to put it in a glass. The whole incident was making me feel increasingly foolish. By the time I walked back, glass of safely anonymous beer in hand, I noticed Muriel Kay Starr seating herself at the next table, *New York* magazine in one fist and planter's punch in the other.

I hadn't seen her in person in years—only photos in magazines of all stripes. At some point in the early eighties she had been the girlfriend of Lila Futuransky, a dyke about town who was later charged with murder but had the charges dropped under mysterious circumstances. Muriel had gone off to the ashram, and that was the last any of us had seen of her until her pictures started popping up in those magazines. David hated her. He was very, very angry about something having to do with something in her books. I just never paid attention when he started to rant and rail. If he hated her so much, why did he follow her so closely?

"This is a community," he used to say. "A community of enemies, and we have to pay very close attention to each other if we want to stay alive."

When she first noticed me she was visibly nervous. She'd gotten pudgy and middle-aged but she still knew how to dress. Her wardrobe revealed hidden wealth. Something nice and simple that fits well and that I've never seen in any store that I can afford to shop in. After an awkward realization of no way out, Muriel accepted that she had to talk to me and we fell into that false intimacy that comes up when you're drinking in a bar. It turned out she was just there by accident having come from a condolence call, so, we did start to talk and I told her David had died.

She was stunned.

"I can't believe nobody called me," she said. "I can't believe Amy never called me."

"Who's Amy?" I asked.

"His publicist. I can't believe no one told me."

At any rate, she ended up telling me a lengthy story about David and the source of their fight. At some moment I started to feel that this might be a historically significant anecdote depending on how much more literary success Muriel Kay Starr was going to have.

This is what she told me.

"I first met David Berman in San Francisco in 1987."

Then she stopped dead in her tracks and ordered a plateful of chicken wings. For the next twenty minutes I had to watch her tearing the meat off those wings with her teeth. She got grease all over her fingers and all over her glass of planter's punch. She got red grease on all the bunched up napkins, pieces of napkin stuck on her fingers and slivers of meat protruding from between her teeth. Then she ordered another planter's punch and another plate of wings.

CHAPTER FORTY-FOUR

"I WAS HAVING A LOVE AFFAIR WITH A MARRIED woman who was teaching at the San Francisco Art Institute and I had traded apartments with a filmmaker living in Cole Valley so that I could be near her. Her husband was back in New York and we spent time together except for holidays like Thanksgiving or Christmas. That's when he would unsuspectingly fly out from New York and stay in her place on Nob Hill at which time I had to basically get lost.

"A friend of mine, Robert, was having an affair with X, a famous gay writer still living, and they were both out in San Francisco since X was touring with his new novel. I was hanging out with them, having been abandoned by my girl and we spent a lot of time talking about AIDS. Especially since Robert's previous boyfriend had died of AIDS and he was extremely paranoid about getting infected. I remember at one point when Robert, who was negative, had been fucking X and the condom broke and Robert was hysterical even though he was the penetrator and X was, himself, negative. It was all at a very high pitch. We weren't all used to it yet.

"One night X, Robert and I were invited to the home of a very wealthy gay man in a mansion in Pacific Heights. He was the brother or cousin, I believe, of the actress who played the Catwoman on the original *Batman*. Every man at the dinner table owned his own vineyard, and each one had brought a bottle of wine from his own stock. A number of them had AIDS, I remember, and one of them had labeled his wine as a benefit for . . . I think it was DIFFA—the designers' AIDS group. Anyway, that night X told me about a young man who had recently interviewed him for *Coming-Up*, the San Francisco gay and lesbian newspaper. And X had been very impressed with this young man and very sad that he had AIDS and was only working on his first manuscript.

"A few nights later we went to a party at the home of Deborah Chasnoff, who would later win an Academy Award for a film about General Electric. And there was this young man we had just been discussing. As soon as X introduced us there was great empathy between us and I felt very close to him. Well, that was David."

By this time the second plate of wings arrived and I watched her devour them again. The smell of lard was deafening. It brought back the embalming fluid of that afternoon and for one moment, I imagined her tearing off David's flesh from his coffin filled with hot sauce and pulling his gristle out from between her teeth. Dipping his celery fingers in blue cheese dressing.

"So David had this manuscript of short stories that he desperately wanted to have published in his lifetime. I took the manuscript home and saw that there were good things in it, even though it was not developed. I remember spending the rest of the holidays, working out my grief at my abandonment by my lover, by enthusiastically editing it."

Polyps of grease were floating in the planter's punch.

They formed lesions on the ice cubes like someone's bad news MRI.

"Well, the story had a happy ending because the book was published, with a little blurb from me on the back, and it did moderately well. But my greatest joy was that David and I were able to read together at The Kitchen the spring after his book was published. I felt that that was a fitting end to our time together because I expected him to die within the year."

She leaned back into the chair, wing in hand.

"But he did not die. He did get sicker, but wrote another book, a novel. Again, it showed promise but wasn't fully developed. Again, I read over the manuscript carefully making editorial suggestions, caring. I remember going to visit him one day at home in New York before that book came out and he could barely walk or swallow. I never expected to see him again. When we talked on the phone some months later, he was terribly upset that his novel was not being reviewed and I quickly called and wrote the *Village Voice* that I desperately wanted to write on this book. I explained by letter twice, and on the phone once, that I wanted the review to come out while David was still alive. About seven more months passed and there was still no answer. Then I saw Stacey, one of the *VLS* editors, on the street and grabbed her, which is a total violation of protocol. She told me that my request was going through the channels and I would just have to wait. Well, the review finally did come out. It was the best review that book got—its only mention outside of the gay press."

She paused then, waiting for me to say something.

"God, you lead an interesting life," I said.

I had no idea of what she was talking about.

CHAPTER FORTY-FIVE

T HE TRUTH IS THAT THE MORE MURIEL KAY STARR talked about this side of David's life, the more I realized I did not know a lot about him. I saw a whiny, kind of wonderful, typically self-obsessed, totally fucked-over gay guy eking out a living in my neighborhood. I saw a lonely, smart guy sitting on a park bench. I saw a loner. Every time I ran into him carrying a bag of groceries, he seemed to be alone.

Muriel, though, was describing this glamorous world of connections and parties, transcontinental affairs, encounters with powerful editors and literary world alliances. Was he like me or was he like her? Was David one of them or one of us?

"And then what happened?"

"Well," she said, waving away the stack of bones. "Wait one minute, I have to go wash my hands."

She came wobbling back a few minutes later and ordered a third planter's punch. I ordered one too and it tasted like Hawaiian Punch and vodka.

"David got sicker and sicker, of course. Time passed and I got a job teaching out in SF for one semester, while he happened to be there. We decided to share an apartment for two months and it went pretty well. He liked to sit in the living room and listen to Joni Mitchell records. He loved to read, discuss books and was an incredible gossip. He had incredibly sarcastic things to say about other people. Some days he was too sick to get out of bed. I would come home from work and he would have been watching all the talk shows all afternoon and recording the most offensive ones. At that time there was a whole series of talk shows about people who supposedly purposely infected others with HIV—these completely infuriated and depressed him. Especially because the shows never mentioned that if everyone would use condoms, these questions would disappear. He would insist that I sit at the edge of his bed and watch his tape compilation of the day's outrages.

"When he finished that novel I did everything I could to help him get a mainstream publisher. I sent it to my own editor and to others, even those I don't have good relationships with. Eventually one of them bought it for two or three thousand dollars. But at the end of our time together I sensed an increasing bitterness on David's part. It wasn't only about his disease and the way his family was treating him. It was something more. Something about the fact that I would live."

I remembered the movies and realized I had twenty minutes to get out of there. I tried easing her to the end of her story and signaled to the waiter for the check.

"When I got back to New York we talked on the phone about once a week. Then he came back too and things seemed to be fine until one day he called and said that he had an in with a good magazine and if he could do an interview with me he would get a regular gig. Of course I agreed. Well, you can imagine how devastated I was to discover that the interview was a hatchet job on my personality. All the things he hated about me that he never said to my face. And there was this profound resentment that a woman could occupy some public space as a respected thinker or intellectual—space that he did not occupy and would never occupy because he was dying. I felt terrible that he violated me so personally and I was disappointed that he proved to be such a jerk about women in the end."

"What did you do?" I asked.

"After the fall he did all the things that weak people do. After attacking me he wanted me to say that it was okay. He called and called and called, leaving millions of messages. And I really had to ask myself if I should overlook this incident because he was dying. For three months I thought about this every day. Finally, I decided that I could not ignore the violation of our relationship. If he was the only dying person in my life, maybe I could be a martyr to his rage—both the justified rage and the unjustified rage. But I am surrounded by dying people and will be until the day that I am one of them and I cannot spend the rest of my life in fake relation. Besides, the anger of men at smarter women is my largest waste of time. But I did write him a letter explaining my decision. This, at least, gave him one last chance to come through."

"Did you ever see him again?"

"No," she said. "But about a month ago I got a letter from his friend Manuel, you know—that Cuban guy—I think he's a poet or something. He had taken my letter and mailed it back to me. Over my writing he had scrawled *you are despicable.* I just assumed that he was taking his rage out on me too. Women are convenient targets for that. Maybe it helped him feel better. And now David is dead. Today was his funeral."

She finished and the check came. We both sat there looking at the piece of paper. I remembered when David showed me an article from *The New Yorker* about the suicide of Sylvia Plath. The author made this really good point about how suicides are always right and those left behind are always wrong.

"But, wait a minute," I said. "Muriel, that's not the only reason that David was mad at you. You're leaving out some very important information."

"Like what?" She seemed exhausted.

"He was mad at you for writing closeted novels. For not even being out in your author bio on the back of the book."

This vocabulary was coming out of my mouth. I was channeling this dead guy and had no proof to back up my argument.

"I am so out. It says there that I've written for *Genre* magazine."

"But what straight person is going to have ever heard of *Genre* magazine?"

"Don't tell me what to do," she said, throwing down a twenty-dollar bill. "David was just jealous. Have you even read my books?"

"I skimmed one."

"David was jealous. You read my book before you complain. It's not about that. My books are not about homosexuality. They're about family. I wasn't even that famous yet and he was terribly terribly jealous."

CHAPTER FORTY-SIX

B Y THE TIME I GOT TO THE MOVIE THEATER, I JUST wanted something to kiss. And, perfect timing—there she was. I spotted her out of the corner of my eye and she spotted me, but she acted like she didn't notice me notice her appreciatively, her light sundress.

Give me polka dots and long tan legs, bare shoulders. Get me away from death and sleaze.

I also noticed that she was with two fags and an old friend on a Friday night so no romance in this girl's life. Nothing important enough for Friday night, anyways.

"Peace for Cuba," I said, flashing a victory sign and she put her hand firmly on the back of my neck like she was going to strangle me, her tiny little kitten. Then she kissed me warmly on the mouth and walked off with her pals. I started to follow but suddenly there was a ruckus behind us and everyone turned around to watch. It was the right-wing gay Cubans making their appearance with leaflets against the films they'd all just bought tickets to see.

Lourdes and her friends sat in one place and I decided to go to the other side since it would be too forward to act that quick. I noticed Manuel, alone, of course, looking totally depressed. I didn't want to sit with him either, so I crawled silently down the aisle behind him without even saying hello.

The films were in Spanish, no English subtitles. I hardly knew anyone there, except an Argentinean Communist who took the seat next to me and immediately started complaining in Spanish about the Cubans.

"They're crazy," he said.

The first short started, but from the beginning the right-wingers couldn't take it. They were mad at anyone who even lived in Cuba. Every time some gay person on the screen had a problem, they clapped. Their Cuba was not allowed even one blade of green grass.

Even though the films were made at an elite Havana film school by elite non-Cuban Latin students, they were all filled with pain. The first three had the same story. A man goes cruising in:

A. a public toilet   B. a movie theater   C. a park

He finds a trick and services him, no reciprocity. Then suddenly they get caught and his lover turns around:

A. yelling "fag"   B. running away   C. beating him up

In one film the lover simply betrayed him without beating him up. It was that place between Stalin and a man's naked body.

Gay movies show where gay people live. I guess gay Cuban men live in public toilets with one-way blow jobs and a lot of stabs in the back, or do they live in those beautiful sanitoriums that the official government AIDS documentary liked to show? The one with fresh orange juice on the table? The whole audience laughed out loud at that one, except for the Anglo lefties who'd gone over with the Venceremos Brigade.

The women's part of the program consisted of ethereal, asexual, femme forms floating in some softcore dimension.

I was sitting in front of the right-wingers and behind Manuel, who sobbed continuously from beginning to end. But the right-wingers were adamant. After each film they would read aloud the names of the people listed in the credits, the list of public enemies. Anyone named after a Communist got a particularly loud wave of scorn.

"Raoul Fidel Troyano," they read out loud in unison. But then a funny thing happened. Every time something really Cuban came on the screen they lurched. Like when one pathetic gay guy in a park offered the other pathetic gay guy a swig from a bottle of Cuban rum. Everyone leaned forward to see the label on the bottle. They wanted to see the details.

Afterwards, I lingered outside and waited for Lourdes and her entourage to emerge. They politely switched to English to accommodate me, so I guessed I was temporarily welcomed into the group.

"That one with the ethereal females," I said. "I didn't get that one."

"I've seen that one twice before," she said. "It had serious lesbian undertones."

She held herself by the shoulders and a shudder ran all through her body like I had her cunt in my lap.

"Let's go home," she said to her friends and then to me. "Do you want to come along?"

"Where are we going?" I asked.

"Anywhere," she said.

"Well, we could just go to your house," I said. "I mean I know I was a jerk to you. I apologize. I know I did the wrong thing. I know I was an asshole. But we both know how good it is going to feel."

Her friends walked on conveniently ahead.

CHAPTER FORTY-SEVEN

LOURDES SLIPPED HER ARM INTO MY ARM AND TURNED around to face me on the street. I thought I was about to be kissed.

"You are an asshole. You are a big assshole. What do you think you are, God's gift to women? You're slime. You think you can just clap your hands and my pussy's gonna crawl?"

"Oh," I said. "You're gonna let me have it instead of just taking me home."

"First I'm gonna call you an asshole," she said. "Then we're going to have sex."

"Oh, okay," I said. "Go ahead then."

She slapped me across the face. Her friends were farther and farther away.

"What's wrong with you, Rita?" she said. "Sexually, you're great. Emotionally, you suck."

"Emotionally?" I shrieked, outraged. "You're the one who doesn't connect. I've never had such a cold fuck in my life. Miss Icy."

"Listen honey," she said. "Why don't we try to really get to know each other?"

"Like a relationship?" I croaked.

"Well, I wouldn't go that far, but I at least think we should go out on a date."

"A date?"

"Tonight we'll have hot sex and then later on in the week we'll go to a museum."

"Okay," I said. "Wednesday?"

"I can't," she said. "I have to go see my son in Union City."

"You have a son in Union City?" I asked. "What is this? Is omission your middle name?"

"Mission?"

"No, omission. You know how fearful people make love—the ommissionary position."

"There's a lot you don't know and can't imagine. Just ask."

"Okay," I said. "I will. That's enough punishment. Can we go home now?"

"My way?"

"Only your way?"

"Only."

"Well," I said. "Right this second my desire for you is larger than everything I know to be true about science and daily life. But if the only way you're going to fuck me is with an unnecessary glove on your hand, then I guess there is nothing I can do about it even though I think it is ridiculous."

"First we go have a drink."

CHAPTER FORTY-EIGHT

S HE ENGAGED ME IN A BRISK WALK AROUND CHELSEA and the more I got dragged along the more I felt out of my element. Like there are two neighborhoods in her neighborhood. One is Spanish and the other is gay. She belongs to both. Going out with her meant sitting in expensive restaurants eating delicious, incredibly overpriced things while she talked to the waiter in Spanish and to the owner in flirtatious arrogance.

"I once came here with a bunch of dykes," she said. "The owner didn't like that. We sat here all through drinks and dinner loudly comparing our cleavages."

After that I didn't know what she was talking about. Something having to do with computers, about how they work.

"What *is* software?" I asked.

She stared blankly.

Okay, so we have nothing in common.

Everything she ordered was incredible. Sautéed mushrooms in garlic and cilantro, crab and avocado salad, gingered oysters. She could talk forever and forever. Ten generations of Spanish aristocracy and two of Cuban aristocracy chatting on the veranda and two of Miami ghettoed bitterness. Some Panama, one Arab, one Jew and a heavy dose of Union City, New Jersey. Astrology, occult, Spanish words I do not know.

I never felt so plain and limited. What a relief. She would be and do everything.

But touching on the street did not feel safe.

"Men bother me every day of my life," I said.

"They don't touch *me*," she said. "I'm like a brick wall."

We ducked into the Rawhide, a greasy men's bar, just on a whim and it turned out to be one of those dens of kind oppression. We could touch and the old queens were drunk and nice. I leaned against the wood like some big dyke and held her by the waist, her arms around my neck. Finally, I liked it.

"I like to be touched," she said. "But not right away. I need to warm up."

By the time we got home it was one happy time. Threw her over my shoulder and down on the bed. She and her music, candles, red wine, fucking bullshit latex gloves, tube of lube, all accoutrement—completely commodified.

"Let's use spit," I said, refusing all purchasable items.

"No. I have my idea. Seduce me."

"What does *seduce me* mean?"

"Go slow," she said. "It's too good to go fast."

Everything I said was what I really felt. Everything I did was what I really wanted. I was never disconnected. I was never in service. It was a two-way street from beginning to end. Fuck a girl in the ass and she's really yours. Her body on your arm like a Popsicle treat.

There was no love between us. None at all and there never would be. There was no understanding. Nothing to talk about. I come from no mobility. She comes from fallen grandeur. She whipped out another round of those silly gloves. We were kissing and I started thinking.

"Aren't you afraid of saliva too?" I said, her tongue in my mouth.

"Your timing stinks," she said. "Your timing is really bad."

"I don't know you at all," I said. "I only know a few things. You're smart and angry and sexy and sad. You're opinionated."

"Opinionated? Me? I know when to keep my opinions to myself."

Later, when my thoughts turned to that night, I had one memory. I am holding her in the morning. All separation between our bodies has been worn down through the night. Everything is quiet now. My hands are on her back and shoulders. Her eyes are cold. She had a faint smile on her lips. I separated her legs and looked at her labia in the sunlight, honking cars and sirens passing outside the window. I eat her, she turns to wax. See, we can make love in the morning, quietly. No pot, no night, no soundtrack from the CD player.

"That's how you tell racial origins," she says later as I fingered her once again. "The darkness at the ends of my genitals."

"Really?" I said, looking at mine. Just pink. It sounded like another theory. Like computers and the stars.

"Really."

And then the memory of David's dad standing in the sunlight came into my head out of nowhere and I realized that I missed my father desperately.

CHAPTER FORTY-NINE

THE FACT IS THAT IN REAL LIFE, NOT JUST ON TV, most teenagers get some kind of family cheerleading when they go out on their first date.

Most of my friends who were straight remember a wistful enthusiasm unless they were Catholic girls with fearful memories. But even then there could be the parading of a new dress before father's tempered approval and a collective anticipation as the first doorbell rang.

"What's he like?" mothers and sisters and neighbors would gossip on grocery checkout lines, and in the Laundromat, about potential boyfriends and cute boys next door.

Even later, after fifteen, when dates were all about drinking and drugs and hand-jobs with skeevy longhairs with bad skin and no future. Even then my friends' beaus would be invited into the living room, shake hands and be forewarned. Encouraging or obstructive, there was a recognition of the importance of these events. Daughters and sons were permitted a kind of preening and exhibition as they measured their desirability in the mirror before Mom and Dad.

For me there was no ritual. There was only secrecy. An institutionalized hiding and deception from the earliest age. My dates were unnoticed. My hopes had to be obscured. As I wondered silently what she would want me to wear, how she would like my hair, what gift would please her, what story, what act. What does she like about me? All the while I had to carry on my life without the slightest hint of its existence.

At dinner Dad would tease Howie about a sparkly brunette named Linda while I ate, silently, tragically, hoping not to be noticed. Eating in a state of rage. The Haases and the Weemses would pass in the hallway with approving comments about nice young couples and decent hardworking girls, young men. I worked hard. I was decent.

But all the time Claudia and I carefully withheld meaning and expression until the sack containing my heart constricted, habitually. I can say honestly that I have never recovered. I am absolutely furious and filled with grief to have had these pleasures taken from me when I was so, so young.

It is just like that scene in Jeanette Winterson's *The Passion* where a young woman leaves her heart back in her married lover's chamber. This event—my love for Claudia Haas and her love for me—is a moment of my personal history in which I have left behind the romantic flights of fancy of a young girl with an open heart. That girl never existed. She was replaced instead by a security guard, a croupier, a study hall monitor, an economist, a soldier, a snake.

My father came home unexpectedly in the middle of the day and found us embracing on his queen-sized bed. Claudia wisely fled. What followed was a murderously humiliating scenario in which my dignity as a human being was erased, permanently, from the family lexicon.

My solitude at this moment. My deep diminishment obscured two facts that would only come to light fifteen years later. First that I did not do anything wrong, even though I was deeply punished. Second, that my father should have been overjoyed that someone loved me and that I loved them. Why should such basic observations—ones available to most straight people without a second thought—elude me until adulthood and then their devastation continue unmitigated?

After walking around the neighborhood, that first afternoon, I took the Seven train into the city and walked around all night. It was 1975. Few homeless people, no crackheads. A young girl could ride the trains and walk the streets with only internal horrors. Looking back now, twenty years later, I see how impossible my flight/exile would be today. I see how much harder, angrier, how much more abused those sixteen-year-old dykes are—roaming around without familial love, late at night. And I also see how much more there is for them now than there was for me. And how little there is for both of us.

CHAPTER FIFTY

IT WAS THE DESIRE TO AVOID DEVASTATION THAT always kept me from calling my dad. Fathers are America's greatest disappointment. Very few of them seem to have done their job. But the ones who came through are so loved. They are adored. The ones who took the time to listen, to ask you questions about yourself, to be happy for you. To actively care.

I have always felt that my father, Eddie, could do that for me anytime he wished. And, frankly, I never understood why he didn't want to because basically I am a terrific person in many ways. I am someone that a father could love.

As my life has progressed, I have changed. I have learned things and come to understand new things. So, it would seem natural that my father would do the same. That's why his abandonment of me has always been a big surprise. Every couple of years, I tried a new approach to see if he could get it. To see if he could get why I am worth loving.

The thing is that now the guy is getting old. Really old. I'm used to death and I think about it casually so I have no trouble knowing that my father will die. My problem is that as long as he is still alive, he has the chance, every second, to change the way he views me. So, every time he refuses, I'm devastated. Because I don't want my father to die with me knowing that he had that chance every day and never took it. How will I be able to live with that for the rest of my life? At least, while he's alive I can hope that he will, someday, try.

Sometimes I wonder what would happen if I ever got a chance to know him. I have a sneaking suspicion that it wouldn't take very long to find out what he was really like. Probably just three or four visits. But it's the not being sure that keeps me crazy. The vague possibility that he might be able to come through fills me, daily, with rage.

I picked up the phone, feeling sick to my stomach, ugly, hateful, repulsive, disgusting. I waited, knowing that I am bad.

"Hello?"

"Hi, Dad?"

"Hello?"

"Hi, Dad. It's Rita."

"Oh, Rita."

I could hear the disappointment in his voice immediately. It devastated me. He was sorry he had picked up the phone.

"How are you, Dad?"

"Everything's fine, everything's fine. Your brother Howie is here with his wife. They're staying here. Howie is washing the dishes right now. Oh, there he goes, turning off the faucet. *Hey Howie, it's your sister.* He's coming over to the phone. Okay, here's Howie."

"Hi Rita."

"Hey, Howie, what are you doing?"

"We're just in town for a few days visiting Dad."

"Are you having fun?"

"Yeah," he said, totally blank. "We took him to Shea last night. The Mets suck."

"Well, have a good visit, Howie."

"Yeah, see ya."

"Bye."

I always keep trying and I always get destroyed. I get destroyed by that father-son bond. What did Howie do to deserve it? When you compare us objectively, he's no better than me. In fact, I have a hell of a more interesting life. And I've been through more, because I was kicked out. So, I know a lot more about living than Howie, who was always in.

What is it with these brothers and sisters of homosexuals? They love that special treatment. They love to take advantage of it. Would it ever occur to Howie to refuse to go to Shea until my dad invited me too? No way. He loves those special rights, those special privileges. You know parental booty is a limited thing. There's just so much money, attention, love, time to go around. Why split it with your queer sibling if you don't have to. Why give up the one thing that makes a regular shmuck like Howie into something special — his normalcy?

That's why we'll never get rid of homophobia in this country. The brothers and sisters of homosexuals have too much at stake.

Phone calls like that set off a whole chain of reactions usually resulting in what I think of as "pain days." Days when I walk around and every time I see families or people with their parents or see any children or hear anyone say the words "my father" or "my mother" I feel transported to Planet Pain. My molecules go there. It is unbearable. Do you know how many kids there are on television? How many families? It's a knife to the throat.

CHAPTER FIFTY-ONE

THAT FIRST NIGHT, AGE SIXTEEN, I STARTED AT Broadway and Forty-second Street at about 9:00 P.M. and walked up the avenue on the east side of the street until I reached 125th. Then I crossed over and walked back down on the west side until I came to Wall Street, about seven miles later. Then I crossed the avenue and did it gain. This first night of refusal—the world's refusal of me—was also the inauguration of the one factor I attribute most prominently to my survival—the institution of systems. I created mental systems to carry me through the punishment of the innocent. I had one pack of Salems, I had twelve hours until morning. That's twenty cigarettes into twelve hours. That's five cigarettes every three hours. That's one cigarette an hour plus two treats. But how to pass the time between? I had to look in the windows of stores until I saw clocks and that search for measured time occupied my mind.

That morning I showed up at high school for the first time in months—washed up in the bathrooms, washing my hair with soap. All day long people stared at me because it was so sticky and wrong. And I slept in the back of the classroom and ate off other people's abandoned lunch trays. A few nights I slept over in school—successfully avoiding the security guards and teachers—stretching out, fully clothed, on those gray industrial carpets. I stared at the fake paneled ceilings and the overflowing wastebaskets filled with leftover lunch. I ate other people's leftover lunch. I developed systems for hunger.

I walked up Broadway starting on the east side and stopped at every restaurant window along the way to read the menus and put together my ideal meal. Appetizer, soup, entree, and salad. Or just pizza with toppings and different time-consuming ways to imagine it. That made the trip last ten times as long and gave me more filler for the hole in my heart. I left my feelings behind. There was Orange Julius.

I went to Nathan's on Fifty-seventh Street and filled plates piled high with free sauerkraut, having one serving with mustard and one without, washed down with abandoned old Cokes and old orange drink. I left my feelings there. A dirty teenage girl sitting alone in the corner of Nathan's nonchalantly sipping on someone else's drink. A shameful person. A disgrace.

I kept going to work in the city and cashing paychecks, washing my hair in Woolworth's shampoo, brushing my teeth in school, walking around on Saturday nights, Sunday nights. The trick in those days was to find a comfortable stoop on a quiet street, maybe on the West Side of Manhattan. There was no competition back then for a quiet spot to sleep.

And I learned through my systems, how to achieve self-hypnosis by staring at car headlights and keeping my mind blank. Sooner or later you forgot you were alive and could zone out that way for up to forty-five minutes. Then, at around 5:00 A.M. it was safe to fall asleep because no one

would be coming by. There were not ninety thousand homeless people then going through every garbage can.

Finally, after a while I snuck back into the building to
Claudia's house. I stared up at my father's window from
across the street and knew he was there but offered nothing.
He did not reach out even though I was the child and he the
adult. When I got to Claudia's her mother was waiting, all
loving kindness. She knew nothing in particular and would
never suspect such a repulsive reality. So, I concocted some
sham story about a family argument, assuring her it would all
be over soon and so, from this—my first confrontation between my homosexuality and the world—I lied from the beginning. I know to this day that I was treated better that way.
I know that lying was the only thing I could do.

CHAPTER FIFTY-TWO

MRS. HAAS WAS COOKING A HOT MEAL. I WAS starving. I wanted it so badly. She chatted away, stirring and stirring and, absurdly, I rattled on about my new life—about all the little details that never happened and the silly conversations that never took place—all the time Claudia looking on with horror because that was the moment that she decided that she did not want to know either. She did not want to know what was happening to me.

I lied continuously, entertaining them, working my way towards that meal, perfecting my systems for keeping people interested enough to feed me. To casually force them to feed me. And just as Mrs. Haas was setting the cracked plates out on the tiny kitchen table, the telephone rang and it was my father, keeping me from my meat.

As he spoke I saw her expression shift to one—not of shock—but registering rather that everything had simply changed. For the second time that week I was humiliated, because I knew that my father had exposed my true and horrendous self to the one person who was offering me a meal.

"I see," she said into the phone, stirring the pot of stew. "I see."

When she hung up the phone she could no longer look at

me. But she did put the meat on my plate. And that was my second lesson about being a homosexual. Not everyone would refuse me, but there would never be a full embrace.

I ate as fast as I could as Mrs. Haas walked off into the other room and sat quietly, alone in the old armchair. I looked at Claudia. She was not my savior.

"I want to go to college," she said.

Claudia's mother made her own peace with the facts and they never came up again. I knew better than to ask to stay over but she did send Claudia to school with extra lunch in her bag for me. Extra tuna fish and hard-boiled eggs chopped up together in a washed-out margarine tub. Extra apple. Claudia and I made love passionately everywhere—in bathrooms, classrooms, elevators. She was in love with me, of that I am still sure. We made love in stairwells, during her lunch hour. She did go off to college, a good one in another town. And I got a second job as a cashier, stealing twenty-dollar bills from the cash drawer to take the train to see her. Terrified, we hid in barricaded dorm rooms and made love with silent terror, not romance. We could give up everything pure and joyous for the one most important desire—to never be caught again.

As Claudia took pre-law and studied in the library keeping up her grades to keep her scholarship and her parents proud, I got a room in the basement of a theater, worked 10:00 to 6:00 at Chuckles and 7:00 to 1:00 at Baskin-Robbins. I ate ice cream for three meals a day and systematically pilfered bananas. I convinced Italian vegetable vendors to let me have their rotten ones. Those were days of no competition for garbage. That night I would cut out the bad sections of each squash or tomato, systematically, and chop the remainders into undifferentiated shreds.

Claudia got an acceptable boyfriend who knew nothing about me. I was expected to go along with all of this, and did, unquestioningly. Finally she confessed to him and he pointed to the passage in the Bible where God says it is wrong. I was utterly alone. She got a new boyfriend after that, became a sophomore. I sold pot to kids from suburbia in Washington Square Park. They weren't afraid of me because I was white. There was no explanation for me. There was no explaining my predicament.

My lying improved enormously. It became quite natural, quite quickly. I got a phony credit card number from an old guy named Adam Purple who handed them out on purple paper from his purple bicycle. I called Claudia from phone booths on cold Greenwich Village street corners. She went to college basketball games. And from that point of divergence, our lives continued apart.

I found out where I belonged and after being turned away from a gay bar for being underage, I managed to get into two or three. La Femme with a fat old man at the door and a suited con walking back and forth across the dance floor. The Dutchess, overseen by Danny of the Israeli mafia, a male bouncer at the door and windows painted black. Black dykes hung out on the west side of Washington Square Park or wandered to Bonnie and Clyde's with the black women downstairs by the pool table and bar and the whites eating pasta in a "women's" restaurant on the second floor. Chaps and Rusty's by Chrystie Street with girls in suits and others in party dresses, the first time I ever socialized with Puerto Ricans. But it was all a game about how long you could avoid the attention of the bartender, while staying constantly on the lookout for some other lost kid who might end up to be that friend I desperately needed.

Afterwards, I could walk over to the pier on West Street and watch the leather queens getting blow jobs or fucking in the open at all hours. You'd walk up and down the aisle and there would be fifty of them. Now, they're ghosts. That's where the gay children were—kids like me with nowhere to go. We sat around listening to someone's radio, and I could lie down at the end of the pier, staring out at old illuminated New Jersey and actually go to sleep knowing I wouldn't wake up raped because gay men don't do that to us.

One night I was so alone. It was my seminal aloneness—every solitary moment since then reminds me of that one spot. Alone with nothing and no one on my side. There was no one out there who was *for* me. And I looked up at a passing boat and saw a rat climbing out of a hole on the dock about three feet from my face. Then I saw that there was a whole swarm of them, that they owned this place and could do as they wished. And instead of running, I just sat there with the rats because there was no other place for me to go.

My first rats. They were the symbol of my condition. And, I have to say, that although it is a blasphemy, I thought of my mother and compared myself to her. We had both been punished and neither of us had done anything wrong. Is it really bad of me to compare myself to a Jew?

Evil is so logical. It is so inventive. The problem is how to keep us out, and the answer is a logical system of solutions. My mother could not go to the same movie theater as her friends. She could not sit on the same bench. She never told me this, but I know it from reading history books. Claudia and I could go but not as what we were, which is lovers. If we wanted to kiss we had to hide in the ladies' bathroom.

CHAPTER FIFTY-THREE

I DON'T GO BACK TO JACKSON HEIGHTS. I HAVEN'T been there in years, not since the Indians took over. I have nothing against anyone, but I need to keep my own little nostalgia intact. Yet, sometimes when the isolation is too great I go up to Eighty-sixth Street and First Avenue and walk around the ruined remnants of Yorkville—Manhattan's version of Kraut-town. My dad told me that my mother used to get dressed up and go over the bridge for some pastry at Cafe Geiger or a copy of the *Aufbau*. Walk past the old Bund building that had been converted into a more benign "gymnasium." Sat on the sidelines watching demure "ex" Nazis marching in the Von Steuben Day Parade. Blondes in lederhosen, with accordions and floats.

For me, I only have one destination—Schaler Und Weber, the smoked-meat deli that still sits there on the corner. I can go in once every couple of years and look over all the different kinds of wursts and sausages. The packaging is still the same from when I was a kid and that smell—that swine smell— brings me back to our tiny kitchen, the old refrigerator, hot summer afternoon windows wide open and neighbors sitting out on the sidewalk in folding chairs. Card tables. Black-and-white TVs. Good books. Thick black bread. Strong mustard.

A glass of beer. Old records, Bach on the scratchy radio competing with someone else listening to the game. The ball game. A rehashed old argument about something that happened back home in a Germany that could never exist again—a paradise. The last place any of these people was Somebody. The last place any of them had a family. The last place they'd ever belonged. Their last good night's sleep. I guess Jackson Heights was my version of Bremen. Now, I too am in exile, staring through a store window in a foreign part of town. I would never buy anything at Schaller Und Weber, though. The taste would be more than I could bear.

"You're David's father, aren't you?" I asked, before I had time to think it over. "I recognized you from the funeral."

I had wandered over to Carl Schurz Park, past that strange strip of Eighty-sixth Street containing the wealthiest of the wealthy, next to pockets of real poverty, a Latin dance hall, a decrepit movie theater, fast food, yuppie bars, leftover working-class white people really looking for trouble. I ended up looking out past the mayor's mansion over the East River from the cool shady park.

"I was just thinking about that," he said. "That park is so far from our house."

What would it have been like to have a father like this one? He seemed so calm and well dressed. Not some stupid slob like my dad. David's father was educated, somewhat genteel. He wore a suit. I hardly ever saw my own father in a suit. Never for the delight of it.

Right away the mechanism of betrayal started up in my brain. Immediately I was burying David, finishing him off, dismissing him, discrediting him. I was blaming him for his family's abandonment. They were upper-class and therefore superior. Why couldn't David have done better with them? I could complete what he had never realized. I had outlived him after all. This was my reward.

And suddenly, it all became clear to me—like one of those moments after years and years of struggle when the thing you've wanted more than anything is sitting safely in your pocket. Suddenly it all seems so easy and right—the order of things.

Now, I lived in a new world, in a new era. The Post–David Era. And, in this world, those of us who remain can move mountains that the dead could never move. I, Rita Mae Weems, could convince his father and therefore own his father. Once I transformed his father, his father would belong to me and then, I would have a father. I could be a daughter. I would finally, because of David's death, get a family. His disappearance had made room for me.

Was this the hidden purpose of AIDS—to give the rest of us a chance to have parents? That was the first explanation I'd come across that could make sense. Maybe these hateful parents would regret the way they abandoned their gay children and would come to other abandoned gay children and love us instead. That way, at least one of us would have love.

CHAPTER FIFTY-FOUR

"I GREW UP OVER MY PARENTS' VEGETABLE STORE," the old man said. "First they had a vegetable cart, and a horse in the backyard. Then they had a vegetable store. This is in Brownsville, East New York. My mother came to America. She didn't know how to read and write. In Russia, she didn't even have her own shoes. I've been sitting here asking myself how I ever got an education when my parents did not know how to read and write. I mean, they could read Yiddish, but not English."

"How did you do it?" I asked, panting.

"My sister. I had an older sister. She was a woman with a will of steel. She was able to wrestle herself from her destiny, despite complete opposition from my parents. They wanted her to go into the family business but she wanted to be a lawyer. In the 1930s! And, in the end, she was the first Jewish woman admitted to New York Law School. But she ended up not going. I don't remember why. I think she didn't have the memory for it or something like that. She became a public school teacher instead. Anyway, that's how I became a lawyer."

Yes, Dad.

"Finished high school, went into the navy and went to City College on the GI Bill. Then I went to New York University Law School and married David's mother during my first year. Believe me, you needed to have a wife to make it through that place. Especially as a Jew. The navy was the first time I really had to live closely with Christians. But law school was an entirely different breed. They had everything going for them. They knew the ropes before they even got there. My wife was working as a public school teacher, just like my sister, and every Sunday we would go out to the old neighborhood and have dinner with my parents. Fricassee, cabbage soup. My whole family came to my graduation. My mother, father, sister, brother, my brother-in-law, my in-laws. The whole day was for me."

Tell me, Daddy. Tell me your dreams. And then when you're done, please ask me about mine.

"That night, my wife and I went for a long walk across the Brooklyn Bridge into the city and all around the town. We talked about what kind of life we were going to have, what kind of children. The son that we would have—David, after my grandfather. And how when he went to law school, he was going to know all the ropes before he got there. At one point, we got to the Hudson River. It was about midnight, and that part of town was very rough then. Old sailors' bars. Don't forget, New York was still an active port. Cobblestone streets. We stood, looking out over the river and a picture came into my mind."

And your daughter?

"I imagined a scene, from my own future. I imagined that my wife and I were older, about the age we were ten years ago. My wife and I are attending the theater accompanied by our son. Broadway. My son and I approach a waiting taxicab from either side of the car. Dapper and fit in crisp tuxedos and tails, you know, like Fred Astaire. I am older than he is, grayer, more elegant and in excellent physical condition. He is impetuous, laughing, handsome. We open the doors simultaneously as our ladies step in before us. His mother, contented, elegant. His wife flirtatious and witty. We glance at each other over the top of the cab before stepping in—two halves of one person. Our unity and similarity are indescribable, unspoken and thoroughly understood. But you see, my dream will never be realized because my son took it away from me the day he decided to be a homosexual."

CHAPTER FIFTY-FIVE

I WAS HAVING AN EXPERIENCE I WAS NEVER MEANT TO have, and it transported me through all kinds of memories and associations, like an Eric Dolphy record—a little bit of this sound and that.

If Dad had asked me what I was feeling I would have told him that these moments leave their mark like a shadow covered in soot. A kind of vain hopefulness rooted in nothing. Like a line of black women in their Sunday best at 6:00 A.M. at the Port Authority Bus Terminal. Children's new clothes, beaded hair, waiting for visits with incarcerated men. Thighs squealing against tight, tight seams and chitchat about caseworkers.

"They come to your house," one says, sipping Coke through a straw, butt encased in a white stretch fabric. "Chantelle, you stop that."

Kids, hopeful. White shoes.

The screaming you hear at home might be from someone else's TV. A live news program feeding your neighbor the original scream, even if the camera's trained on you.

"What did you lose?" I asked. "What did David take away from *you*?"

"Normalcy," he said. Old, stupid man. "I had strange

parents, don't forget that. They had accents. They could not read or write. They weren't educated. They didn't understand anything. My sister wanted to be a lawyer, but for her generation, that was not normal. It was not normal for women to stand out that way. I was the son. I was the first one in my entire family to be appropriate. What is so awful about being appropriate? About making something of yourself? David had to be a big shot. He had to be oppositional. And look where it got him."

He looked at the ground. I didn't know if he meant *hell* or *six feet under.*

"It is bad enough that he had to be homosexual, that he had to do that to me. But then he had to write about it so everyone in the world would know that our family was not normal. My son went to Columbia University and he spent his life writing pornography. Do you know what he used to call me? David Greenglass! Can you imagine. Calling your own father David Greenglass?"

"Who is David Greenglass?"

"Oh, you must not be Jewish. You've heard of the Rosenbergs, Ethel and Julius?"

And for the first time, he asked me a question and waited for the answer, really wanting to know.

"Of course."

"Ethel was sent to the gas chamber by the testimony of her own brother. Ethel Greenglass. After his sister was executed, he was disappeared into a witness protection program. You know, the FBI changed his name and set him up in a little house somewhere. Actually, you have to pity the man. How he must have paid. This is what my own son calls me — like I am sending him to his death. One day my daughter and son-in-law and I decide to go out to the movies. We go to see Woody Allen's *Crimes and Misdemeanors*. We're standing on line and who else is there waiting to get in? David. My son. He was alone, so of course, we invite him to it with us and he was sitting next to me, just like he used to when he was a little boy. Sitting next to me in the dark. We're watching the film and then Woody Allen makes a joke. He says, 'I love you like a brother, like David Greenglass.' And David, my son, starts to laugh and laugh. He's laughing too loud and everyone is looking at us. It was one of those audiences where no one else got the joke. And I knew he was laughing at me. Good for him. He laughed and now he's dead. And I'm not laughing."

"No."

"Near my first law office was an old cafeteria called Cohn's Cafeteria. Not Roy Cohn, but another Cohn. And we would sit there in Cohn's watching Roy Cohn drive by in his chauffeur-driven limousine. I knew this attorney, Ernie Kaufman, not like Judge Kaufman, the Rosenbergs' judge, but a different Kaufman. Ernie. We sat with Cohn—the cafeteria Cohn, not Roy Cohn, and Ernie told us that he had to sue Roy Cohn for some client and the guy didn't have a cent. Even with those chauffeurs. Cohn. Kaufman. Greenglass. They were all after something. Something big. But so were Ethel and Julius. Two factions of the same tribe. They wanted influence. All of them. I, personally, never needed to make an impact. I just wanted the best for my children."

Breeze.

"One time he came to my office."

"Cohn?"

"No."

"Kaufman? Rosenberg? Greenglass?"

"No, no. My son. He was demanding to know why I wasn't ecstatic that he was a homosexual. 'What do you want?' I asked. 'Some parents don't even let their children into the house. I always let you into the house.' I wasn't the worst."

"But, Dad," I said. "What about love?"

"Listen," he said. "I love my son. I have always loved my son. I have always been there for him. Any time he ever needed anything he always knew that he could count on me."

CHAPTER FIFTY-SIX

I SPENT THE NEXT THREE DAYS GOING TO KILLER'S house straight from work. Troy and Killer and I would sit around eating spaghetti in front of the television set or having soy milk in our coffee and other healthy stuff. No dairy.

"What's new at work?" I asked Troy.

"It is mob-action on the streets, as usual. Outside, everyone is rollerblading. The whole city. Every time I buzz someone into the bakery, they arrive up the three flights of stairs panting like crazy because they're wearing rollerblades. And those helmets and knee caps. All in shiny black, if you have good taste. Everyone under twenty-five looks like an ad for the Gap or Guess Jeans. And, you know what else?"

"What?"

"Those people who tattooed and pierced ten years ago to set themselves apart from mainstream society?"

"Yeah?"

"They've gotten sucked back in against their will because every slob from the suburbs has a modified body these days, but since it's all permanent, the originators can't distinguish themselves from the conforming mass."

"What's gonna be next?" I asked.

"Amputation," Killer said. "It's obvious."

"I don't know," Troy speculated. "Probably they'll all become born-again Christians or Goddess worshipers. There's nowhere to go but out of the body."

"Well, the leather queens and kings have really changed the world," I said.

"Yeah," Killer added. "Now every housewife in America can wear her chaps to the mall."

"Thank God the grunge look is in," I said. "Now I can look like a seventies lesbian and be totally on the money."

"Rita," Killer whined. "You're soooo over. Grunge was out the day it appeared in the Style section of the *New York Times*. The happening thing now are the Crusties."

"Crusties?"

"Yeah, you know. Those kids on Avenue A encrusted in dirt. They sleep in piles on the corner of Ninth Street."

"Oh, you mean the ones who say, *'Could you please spare some change so I can buy drugs?'* "

"Yeah," Troy said. "The pierced-forehead set."

"But, honey," Killer added. "Don't confuse them with Riot Grrls. They are really sexy. But they don't seem to be interested in older women."

"Maybe we should start the Woman/Girl Love Association," Troy suggested.

"Well, if they stay in this neighborhood long enough we'll meet them all eventually." Killer sighed.

"I don't know why I'm ragging on these kids," I said. "I mean, I've had a tattoo since 1980."

"What is it?" Killer asked. "A woman on the moon?"

"Well, just be glad it's not a woman's symbol. Or Mr. Natural."

"Well," Troy said. "It's not enough to just have a tattoo.

It has to be something like computer bars on your face. You know, something dramatic."

"Well, dykes are doing heroin again," Killer announced. "That's pretty dramatic."

"I guess not dying of AIDS puts a lot of pressure on people." Troy laughed.

"What do you think is gonna happen?"

"Well," Troy answered, knowingly. "Everything will be fine and then someone will die and then everyone will go to AA except two people will never go to AA. Something like that."

Then we watched TV for a while and talked about other things.

CHAPTER FIFTY-SEVEN

It was Troy's idea to go spy on Claudia Haas. She made a few phone calls, with me standing over her shoulder, and amassed a huge amount of information in no time flat. Turns out Claudia was living with her husband and kid in a suburb of Wilmington, Delaware. The plan was so easily apparent that I began to worry.

"I'm dead set against it," I said, unconvincingly.

But Troy was already plotting her adventure and went out with Killer to buy rice cakes and trail mix for the car trip down.

When they left me alone in the apartment I was agitated, nervous. The truth is that I wanted a happily-ever-after with Claudia—not a shoot-out to the death. It wasn't making a fool out of myself that worried me—I was used to that. The major thing I feared was having to face all that pain. Having to really relive it.

As a diversion, I started reading Muriel Starr's novel, which was sitting, unfinished, on Troy's pile of things to take care of someday. By the end of chapter four, I was convinced that this trip was something I absolutely had to do.

Troy came back with maps and a flashlight. She turned out to be the only one among us with a driver's license, but no one had a credit card. Then, I remembered that Lourdes had about six of them, and surely one or two would not be maxed out. So, I called her up and she was surprisingly nice about the whole thing.

"The truth is I have nothing better to do," she said. And then agreed to use her AmEx to rent a car from Budget Rentals.

I guess we were all feeling lethargic and slightly ludicrous. Everyone around us was complaining that things were hearkening back to the fifties with great rapidity, but from my point of view the nineties looked worse than the fifties had ever been. The main difference having to do with the total absence of enthusiasm, excitement and hope. False hope is better than none at all. So, whether you had an analysis of why or just went for it — anything seemed like a viable out. We were desperate. Desperadoes waiting in line for an opportunity — and the line went on forever with no one at the other end.

Since everything was on the spur of the moment, we couldn't get it all together to leave until after dinner on Friday night, so Troy took the car out for little practice spins while we waited for Lourdes to get out of work. Then we picked her up in front of the computer store and the four of us drove out on our way to Delaware.

The traffic out of the city was unbelievable, especially since there was a water main break on the FDR, which we had taken for speed purposes, even though I would have rather just gone through the streets.

Sitting there overheating I caught a little spark of happiness as I hooked into the romantic angle on all of this. Seeking out your lost love.

There's a special movie star feeling driving through the neighborhoods of New York City on a summer night. Everyone is outside, all those Dominican men with their cotton shirts open and women sitting on stoops and folding chairs. Radios. Water streaming from fire hydrants. Kids, jumping in front of the car chasing balls, so you have to be on alert at all times. Everyone's got a Budweiser. The garbage never gets picked up. Sirens. Yellow lights from hallways, open windows with TVs flickering unattended in the background. Dogs without leashes. Skinny legs on small boys. Pir Agua for the Latinos, and greasy meat on skewers for everyone else.

I told Troy to just take the regular streets until we got to Jersey, but she wanted to take the Drive because she said she liked to merge.

So, we ended up in the middle of incredible congestion somewhere around South Street Seaport. Between the cars and the cabs and the tourist buses, you couldn't move a muscle. Plus, all those Americans and their families dodging in and out. Thank God for South Street Seaport. Now, when Americans come to New York they have a place to go. Everything is the same as their luxury malls back home and it keeps them all together in one spot.

"So," Troy said, cigarette hanging out of her mouth like the guy actor in all those serial killer movies.

"So?" I asked.

That was a provocation because we all knew Troy had fucked up already and we were still in Manhattan. So, then she had to jab back at me by reminding us about the whole purpose of these travels.

"So, how did Claudia Haas get from here to there?" Troy asked as we waited out the crush.

"I told you. She got married six months after we broke up."

"Who'd she marry?"

"Some guy. Some guy she met in sophomore economics. Some guy from a fucked-up family with a real income. You know, someone normal. Who knows? She was only twenty-one."

"You think that's young?" Lourdes asked incredulously.

"Look, not one of the girls I grew up with got married at twenty-one. We're talking the mid-seventies here. You have to think back. We're talking the days when there were no more proms in the high schools and boys had to take Home Ec. You know, the last gasp of consciousness before the disco years."

"You know what ruined it all?" Killer said, wiping the sweat from her face. "That moment that Sha-Na-Na stepped on the stage at Woodstock. That was the beginning of fifties nostalgia and the end of everything new."

"I'm sick of nostalgia," Lourdes said.

"Not me," I said. "I have nostalgia every day. Usually for some moment an hour or two before when I felt okay."

"Well, I'd like to see some Joni Mitchell nostalgia," Killer said. "Fuck Led Zeppelin."

"You're right," Troy said. "College girls in the seventies did not get married at twenty-one. Most of them are just getting married now."

"Sounds like a panic marriage to me," Lourdes said. "I know about that."

"Why, are you married?" I asked.

CHAPTER FIFTY-EIGHT

WE SAT THERE STEWING IN THE HEAT AND TROY smoked a couple more butts.

"Claudia's still with that guy," I said suddenly.

"Maybe she's the kind who falls in love forever," Killer answered.

"But that's the whole thing," I said. And at that moment all the pain started coming through. Like it started in my upper arms, a kind of sharp anxiety, and the saliva in my throat went stale. It turned.

"If she could stay with that guy all these years, well, it seems logical that if no one had bullied us the way they did—I mean, if we had had somewhere to go—we might be the combination who were still together."

I was really angry now. But I was quiet. Killer and Troy know me so they knew to say nothing, but Lourdes doesn't know me from a hole in the wall.

"Don't be too dramatic," Lourdes said, puffing out the window. "You'll never know what Claudia would have been if she didn't have a reason to get married. Besides, straight people have problems too, you know. If my mother ever caught me in bed with a boy she would have thrown me out on my ass."

"Yeah, but," I said, getting really furious, really fast and absolutely hating her. "You would still have had something. You would have had an idea. You would have had an image of young love, an image of romance, of just the two of you against the world. You would have had a friend or a romantic adult who looked at you and saw Romeo and Juliet, instead of just the two of you totally alone looking at each other and seeing nothing."

"Okay," Troy said. "You're not going to believe this but I think we're almost out of gas."

"I told you not to go to Budget," Lourdes said.

Killer started fiddling with the radio.

"Pull into that Esso station over there," she said. "I remember it from when I was a kid."

"Esso?" I laughed. "You've got to be kidding. It is called Exxon now, Killer. Where the hell have you been?"

"I don't usually ride in cars."

"You're just the consummate New Yorker, right?" I said, still mad at Lourdes. "You call the R train the RR train and you call the L train the LL train and you call Avenue of the Americas Sixth Avenue, and you remember where Klein's used to be."

"We're definitely in need of gas."

Troy pulled onto a side street and we started driving around looking for a gas station.

"The thing I want to know," Killer said, "is what Claudia thinks about *you*."

"Yeah, me too," I said.

"I bet homosexuality and you are linked forever in that girl's heart."

"Hopefully she's not the only one who feels that way."

"Oh-oh," Lourdes said. "We have an ego here, out of control. Somewhere east of the Cherry Street projects."

CHAPTER FIFTY-NINE

W E'RE STUCK IN CHINATOWN," TROY SAID, having transplanted us into the same kind of chaos but with a completely different cast. Shopping bags of vegetables, everywhere you turned. Dirty fish on melted ice.

"West Side Highway," Lourdes ordered. "Take me there immediately."

"Chinatown," Troy said, suddenly in some form of reverie and not at all bothered. "Is this the way to suburbia? I can't figure out how to get there."

"Obviously," Lourdes snorted.

"I mean, I don't know how to get out of *here*."

"Same difference."

"No," Killer said, back on her own track. "What *I* mean is that, okay, this girl Claudia opted out of the whole deal because she could not imagine a world where there would ever be a place for a queer vision of herself. But, as Gomer Pyle said, *surprise, surprise, surprise.*"

"Yeah, the world has changed," Lourdes said.

"Thanks to people like us," I said.

That shut us all up, because it was so true. And sitting in traffic somewhere on Mott Street, us four little dykes were suddenly proud of ourselves and the work that we had done to make this world a better place for everyone else.

"Gee, you guys are the best," I said.

"Well, it hasn't changed that much," Killer added. "I just remembered everything homophobic that has ever happened to me."

"Oh, every minute of every day? Don't think about that now. We were having a weepy moment of delusion."

"Well, it's half true," Lourdes said. "Every night now when Miss Thing turns on the TV she has to see *you*. Every day when she opens up the newspaper there is some sign of *you*. Every time she goes to a dinner party, something about *you*, Rita, just happens to come up. You and the military, AIDS and you, you in the movies, you on *Roseanne*. Try as she might, that bitch cannot get you out of her mind."

"Finally," Troy said, pulling into a beat-up station at the end of Fourteenth Street right by the West Side Highway.

There were desperate crackheads running around without shirts or shoes. There was the usual army of working girls flashing plastic tit and lots of dykes lining up across the street to get into the Clit Club.

"Is it midnight already?" Killer asked. "Well, we'll get to her street just in time for the milkman and the paper boy."

"Cash or charge?" the attendant asked and we all looked at Lourdes.

"You know I'm good for it," I said, rather unconvincingly and then wondered if I had become one of those people who used other people for their credit cards.

"Whatever," she said just when I had anticipated a snappy comeback.

So we sat in the car waiting for the attendant to come

back and all looked out the windows at the lesbians hanging out in front of the club.

"It's a new generation," Troy said finally. "Our kind are old meat. They're not better or worse. Just new."

"They're freer," Killer said. "But not enough."

Then the attendant came back with a pissed-off attitude.

"I had to take away your card," he said, handing back the two broken pieces of green plastic. "I can't give you the gas until you pay."

We sat there in the car for a moment or two, each looking out one of the windows. The bouncer at the Clit Club was making men stand on line. One man for every seven girls. A bunch of guys in suits showed up trying to get in. We knew there was no way they were going to get in. This was the only place on earth where they were not going to get in.

"I guess I don't really need to go to the suburbs," I said.

"Well, we'd better take the car back so Lourdes doesn't get in trouble," Killer added, softly.

"I'm already in so much trouble, it really would not make a difference."

The suits across the way could not believe they weren't getting in. They couldn't get over it.

"Look at those girls," Troy said. "They are so young. When I was that age I promised myself I would never be conventional. My life would never be predictable. I would never stop noticing people and their places, streets."

"Your wish came true," Killer said.

"Let's take back the car and go have a beer," I said.

"Okay," everybody said, but they said it sweetly.

Then Troy got the car back to the lot with the needle on empty.

APPENDIX

GOOD AND BAD

BY MURIEL KAY STARR

GOOD AND BAD
by Muriel Kay Starr

Chapter One

"DAVID'S TONGUE IS LIKE THE BUTCHER'S," RITA TOLD CLAUDIA ON the phone. "You remember, the one on Eighty-second Street in Jackson Heights?"

"Mr. Braunstein," Claudia said. "But do you mean that bloody raw cow's tongue he always seemed to be slicing on the counter? The wooden counter? He gave us pieces of baloney. They tasted so waxy and sweet. Like warm chocolate pudding made from scratch. The pudding was grainy, like the meat."

"No," Rita said. "I mean the tongue in Mr. Braunstein's mouth."

"Like *The Sign In Sidney Braunstein's Window*? It sounds like the title of an off-Broadway play."

"Oh, how is the play going?"

"Oh God, you want the latest career news?"

"Of course, you know I want to know everything that happens in your life."

"Well," Claudia said. "One weekend only, in the basement of the Village Gate. A cute TV sketch about the U.S. Open. First, let us settle the question of the tongue."

"Okay," Rita said. "I remember going into the butcher shop with my mother. You know it is one of the few memories I have of her."

"I know," Claudia said. "But I don't know the part about the tongue."

"He had this incredible mouth," Rita told her. "Sexy and huge. I remember I used to watch it, dripping with saliva. Coated in slime. This is when I was still in the stroller, probably sitting there drooling myself. His tongue was enormous. Greasy. It was chewy. That's what David's tongue is like, since you asked."

"What is the daily husband update?" Claudia asked.

"Oh, God, I feel so bad for him. David works harder than anyone I know, but he just can't get a break. You know how hard it is for white men to get jobs in academia these days. It just breaks my heart. It's weird, but now that we're married, I feel everything that happens to him as though it was happening to me. I wonder if that will happen to you when you get married."

"I don't know," Claudia said. "I just don't feel a need to get married yet. I just don't have a good reason. Hey, don't you have to go to work?"

"Oh God," Rita said, realizing the time. "I'm glad you know my schedule. I gotta get out of here."

"Where are you tonight? Becker or McAdams?"

"Becker gave me a week of nights."

"That's good. Higher rate."

"Yeah, and there's no night manager so the word processors can go home at midnight and bill for full-time. As long as they don't realize that we are smarter and therefore faster than they think we are, we'll never get caught."

"Okay, go to work."

"Okay, honey, talk to you tomorrow. David and I will come see your show on Saturday night."

Rita knew that she was late again and raced out of the apartment, trying to run down the stairs and button her coat at the same time, which of course did not work. So, she stopped on the next landing to set the buttons right and could hear the intercom buzzing through the door in apartment ten.

"Lourdes?" the muffled voice called up. "It's Manuel. You want to go out for coffee?"

That's nice, Rita thought. A friend stopping by on the spur of the moment. A friend in the neighborhood who just happened to think of you. To think of your face on the other side of a nice warm cup.

Chapter Two

EDDIE WEEMS WAS A NIGHT OWL. EVEN AT THE AGE OF SIXTY-NINE, HE never went to bed before five in the morning. All those years of working night shifts. All those years of walking out into the cool evening breeze to begin when everyone else was in retreat. Owning the night. Ending your day with whatever you want for breakfast and beginning it with an evening shower and an after-dinner shave.

Jimmy Hoffa had been his man. They'd fought so hard to join the teamsters. Watched their guy stand up to those Kennedy snots. But now, at the moment of truth, all the Teamsters ever did for Eddie was a $288 monthly pension and a social security check. So, why adjust to living by day? Day is too expensive. Night is cheap. There's nothing going on but a drive or a walk or a long slow drink in a quiet bar. There a television show, an old leftover newspaper, let some other Joe pay the fifty cents. The waitresses are chattier at night. The cops are tireder. The cabbies are lonelier. The radio is weirder. There's less traffic everywhere you look.

Now, even his daughter was working at night. Working at night and living by day—letting go of the stresses of the nine-to-fivers. There's a lot less to compete with at 4:30 A.M.

"Rita, line four. Rita, line four."

"Hello?"

"Hi kiddo, what's doing?"

"Entering the copy for an in-house marketing plan."

"Oh yeah? What are they selling this time, those crooks?"

"Drugs."

"You working for the Mob now, Rita?"

"No, Daddy, it's a pharmaceutical advertising firm."

"I'm telling you they always think up some new kind of way to make money. Whatever happened to . . ."

"What are you doing, Dad? Wait . . . I've just got to save this. Okay, what are you doing?"

"I'm just sitting here, naked, wondering what my daughter is doing."

"Dad!"

"What do ya want? The heat is up too high."

"So turn it down."

"Listen, hows about taking your dad out for breakfast? When are you getting off? Take me to that all-night Chinese for some salt-and-pepper scallops."

"I'm getting off at midnight."

"I'll pick you up, sweetheart. Just tell the night guard that your boyfriend is coming to pick you up."

"Dad."

"I'm telling you," he said at 12:32 over a dirty Formica table and two Budweisers at Wong Fat's Twenty-Four-Hour Chinese. "No matter what kind of fancy labels we put on our beer—nothing will ever beat those beers we had in London during the war. They call them pints. Like half a quart but in a really big glass. And warm. The girls couldn't keep off of me. Those English girls, they knew how to have a good time. Especially with a GI. They love us over there. Those cozy nights with no electricity and everything still. You have some of those pints and hope you're in the right place at the right time when the lights go out. Lights Out! Man, oh man, those were the two words I longed to hear. Hey Charlie, how about some service over here?"

A tired, old Chinese man looked up from a tired, old Chinese newspaper and snapped at his son behind the counter. New Jack Chinese happening dude with black fashions and white haircuts. Reading *VIBE* magazine, and some other publication for the all-American Asian homeboy.

"Gimme those salt-and-pepper scallops," Eddie said. "This is my daughter here. She's taking her dad out for breakfast."

"What do you mean, salt-and-pepper scallops?" the kid asked.

"You know," Eddie said, frustrated already. "Salt and pepper. Salt and pepper. With that special sauce."

"I don't know," the kid said. "Is it on the menu?"

He wiped off the table and then wiped off the menu and Eddie started reaching around for his glasses.

"I can't see a thing," he said, patting his empty breast pocket.

"Dad, you still didn't get new glasses?"

"I didn't have a chance," he said. "Rita, take a look at the menu."

"Garlic Scallops, Deep Fried Scallops, Scallops in Black Bean Sauce, Sautéed Scallops, Ginger Scallops."

"That's it, sautéed. Salted. I'll have the salt-and-pepper scallops. So how's that husband of yours? Waiter, bring me a fork and a knife."

Chapter Three

SITTING ACROSS THE TABLE FROM HER FATHER FILLED RITA WITH A terrible sense of loss. Like something was forever moving out of her arms. Like her mother off to the hospital, leaving Rita alone forever. Like her mother on a train to Thereisenstadt, leaving Germany behind forever. Her youth, gone, forever.

Rita tried to make peace with these events in a self-aware contemporary way. She tried to confront them, amassing a sea of facts. Surprisingly, these facts helped everything make sense. But, eliminating the mystery did not make peace. Understanding does not make peace. Facing facts does not bring peace.

Here were the facts, unearthed in secret over the years in many libraries, bookstores and magazine racks.

The German Reisburo ran the passenger trains and they also ran the deportation trains. Both on the same system. Full-fare for adults, half-fare for children, free for children under four. Little children rode free.

But the problem with their ticketing system was that passengers bound for internment or extermination only required one-way tickets. And so the Nazis had to come up with a financing plan to substitute for the cost of the unfulfilled return trip. Correctly, they hit on the idea of seizing prisoners' belongings to pay for the train travel.

Now, this fact could not help Rita understand her own life, because it was a fact that her mother, Louisa, never even knew. So, in many ways it was an irrelevant fact. When the historian knows more than the victim, there is an isolation from the original experience. An isolation reenforced constantly by too much information of the wrong kind.

At this point of revelation Rita abandoned a further search for facts, hoping instead to stumble on the core of meaning filled with explanation—not about the course of history, but instead on the course of her own emotional legacy. Her own future. The meaning was buried, somehow, in the process of a group of men in military uniforms or civilian dress, sitting down over coffee or at a conference table and trying to solve the problem of funding those return tickets. The logic of it. Proposing various other plans and then dismissing them before hitting upon the right one. The most practical one.

As she sat across the table from her father, Rita confirmed, yet again, her own quiet belief that her mother deliberately married a man who would never ask himself any of these questions. He would accept facts of history as facts, and have certain predictable beliefs about the grossest rights and wrongs. But when it came down to individual proposals for solutions to socially symptomatic questions, Rita's mother picked a man who was incapable of transcending. She wanted it that way. Because she didn't want to know. And he would never know. Rita, therefore, must know. But she must never, ever tell.

"Your brother Sam is really trying to make it out there in LA."

"I know, I talked to him last week."

"Going to the gym every day."

"That's what you gotta do, Dad, if you want to make it in that world."

"You gotta look the part," he said. "I'll tell you . . ."

While he was talking Eddie held up his knife, the one he'd been using to cut the scallops. And he waved it in the air to make a point about Sam, but suddenly it was like the whole dinner had ceased to exist and Rita was transformed back to Jackson Heights on a warm summer night in 1975 when her father came at her with a knife. A knife covered in mayonnaise. A knife glistening in grease from a tunafish sandwich.

"You whore," he said. "You slut, fucking some Puerto Rican in your old man's bed. You dirty, dirty whore. I fucked girls like you when I was in the army. Girls like you are a dime a dozen."

"You know, Dad," she said, back in Wong Fat, keeping her eye on that greasy knife. "Guys who want to make it are a dime a dozen. Sam needs that extra edge."

"Well, if he can get it in the gym, God bless him," Eddie said, returning easily to his plate. Drawing blood from his plate.

Chapter Four

HE WAS YELLING SO LOUDLY THAT MRS. HAAS CAME RACING DOWN THE
stairs to sweet-talk Eddie out of murdering his kid.

"Eddie," she said seductively in her Berliner accent, whispering
him into her kitchen. Serving him some coffee and homemade *apfel
kuchen*. "Eddie, she never had a mother. She never had a mother."

"I know," he said. "But what can I do?"

"It's a new world, Eddie," Mrs. Haas said, another well-bred
German Jew whose destiny had eluded her, trapped now with these
working-class slobs in this bland boring neighborhood. She patted
him on the back and served another piece of cake. "You're the only
family she's got."

"But what do I know about girls?" he said.

Rita and Claudia stood in the hall outside the apartment, listening in through the open door. They stood together, silent and still, and
Rita thought about her mother waiting to be arrested. Standing de-
murely in her grandfather's foyer, standing politely as she had been
taught to do. Waiting. And Rita knew that her destiny lay in this moment—not because of her exposed sexuality, her naked body with
their boy. Not because of the threat of violence. But because this was
her chance to have someone love her. This was her chance for Mrs.

Haas to invite her to come live upstairs and be part of them. Claudia's sister was getting married, there'd be room in Claudia's bedroom. There would be room for Rita to be part of their family. Please God, invite me. Please God, invite me. Please God, invite me.

"What do you think he's going to do?" Claudia whispered quietly, flat against the wall.

But Rita couldn't answer. Her desire was too palpable. Please God, invite me. Please God, invite me.

Finally her father came out into the hall, looked down at the floor and walked past them silently. Rita waited for Mrs. Haas to come out into the hall. She didn't dare enter the tiny apartment because she wanted to so badly, she wanted to live there.

"This is silly," Claudia said, finally relaxing. "It's over now. Anyway, you're going to be late for work."

Claudia stepped into the apartment, leaving Rita in the hall. She waited another five minutes, staring at the closed apartment door. She was devastated. She couldn't believe it. Rita had been so sure they would invite her into the family. She had been so sure.

"Tell me, Rita," Mrs. Haas said one afternoon as the two of them met at Mr. Braunstein's butcher shop. "What is it in your life that you most want to avoid?"

"I don't want to live in Jackson Heights," Rita said. "I want to live in Manhattan."

"Well then you'd better get a good job," Mrs. Haas said. "A pound of liverwurst, please."

"How do I do it?" Rita asked, desperate. "How do I get a good job?"

"Mr. Haas says the future is in computers. Computers are the jobs of the future."

Rita was desperate. There were only a few minutes left. She had to get everything she needed for her entire life out of these few minutes. It was the only love she was ever going to have. Love being informative attention.

"How do I find out about computers?" she asked breathlessly.

The next day a quiet envelope was slipped underneath her front door. Course listings and the number for financial aid. When Rita got her masters in computer graphics she sent Mrs. Haas a card at her retirement community in Florida. Same for her wedding to David last spring.

"That was superb," Eddie said, balling up his napkin and pushing away the plate, placing his loaded knife haphazardly by its side. There was something in his knife that reminded Rita of her life. That reminded Rita of that night. That terrible night. When she came so close to getting what she needed, what every child deserves. Someone to be on her side. Someone to defend her. That night when she lost everything, that night that was still on her hands.